THE PRINCE OF EGYPT

DESTINY AND DELIVERANCE

SPIRITUAL INSIGHTS FROM THE LIFE OF MOSES

PHILIP YANCEY

MAX LUCADO

JOHN C. MAXWELL

JACK HAYFORD

JONI EARECKSON TADA

TOMMY BARNETT

KENNETH BOA

THELMA WELLS

Publishers Since 1798

THOMAS NELSON PUBLISHERS
Nashville

Library of Congress Cataloging-in-Publication Data

Destiny and deliverance / Philip Yancey ... [et al.].
      p. cm.
    ISBN 0-7852-7018-3 (hardcover)
1. Moses (Biblical leader) 2. Prince of Egypt (Motion picture)
I. Yancey, Philip.
BS580.M6D47 1998
222'. 1092--dc21   98-39382
                              CIP

Printed in the United States of America.

1 2 3 4 5 6 — 03 02 01 00 99 98

CONTENTS

INTRODUCTION

he biblical story of Moses is powerful and timeless.
It echoes with profound themes such as those sug-
gested by the title of this book: *Destiny and
Deliverance.* It was Moses' personal destiny to lead the
Hebrews out of Egyptian bondage. When Moses

was only a baby, God saved him from Pharaoh's death sentence so
that he could fulfill that destiny. God then filled Moses' life with
many rich and remarkable experiences that served him well as God's
appointed deliverer. In the Exodus account, God also fulfilled the
destiny of the Hebrew people by preserving them and their faith
and leading them to "a land flowing with milk and honey" (Ex.
3:17 NKJV), just as He had promised He would.

Moses' story is, of course, intimately connected with the history
of the Jewish people, particularly with the account of their deliverance. After four hundred years of bondage, the Lord announced to
Moses that the time had come to set His people free. He explained,

"The cry of the children of Israel has come to Me, and I have also seen the oppression with which the Egyptians oppress them . . . I will send you to Pharaoh that you may bring My people, the children of Israel, out of Egypt" (Ex. 3:9–10 NKJV). The account of Moses' life is an amazing record of the powerful and personal ways in which God intervened to deliver His people.

Thousands of years later, we still find in the story of Moses inspiration, drama, and valuable life lessons. The animated film *The Prince of Egypt* presents his story to a new generation in a way never before possible. And in this book, beloved Christian authors reflect on Scripture and the film to help you explore the power and the significance of Moses' story.

Each contributor focuses on a key theme or event in Moses' life, considering its importance in Moses' time and in today's world. Each chapter reflects the unique voice of its author as well as the uplifting spirit of the film. The book offers rich spiritual insights to help you get the most out of the film and to enhance your understanding of the significance of the biblical account.

Destiny and Deliverance also features beautiful four-color art that inspired *The Prince of Egypt.* Each piece was chosen from more than four thousand pieces of development art, which was created to establish the overall visual style and mood of the film and in some cases the color palette for a given sequence. The original art was executed in various media, including oils and acrylics, and varied greatly in size, with some pieces measuring only two inches by three inches. We hope you enjoy the art we've selected. Through it, you will get a rare glimpse of the stunning creative work that takes place before animation ever begins.

May *Destiny and Deliverance* enrich your life, lift your spirit, and broaden your vision.

THOMAS NELSON PUBLISHERS

THE FAITHFULNESS OF GOD IN KEEPING HIS PROMISES

TOMMY BARNETT

*Tommy Barnett illustrates that,
like Moses, we are able to experience God's
faithfulness by acknowledging
and responding to His presence in
our everyday lives.*

The Faithfulness of God in Keeping His Promises

magine Moses centuries ago, standing upon the heights of Mount Sinai, holding the tablets of the Ten Commandments, eyes alight as he gazed on the landscape below. It was the promised land— the land secured by the clear word of God: "God is not a man, that He should lie, nor a son of man, that He should repent. Has He said, and will He not do? Or has He spoken, and will He not make it good?" (Num. 23:19 NKJV).

Because he had firsthand experience with the God of Abraham, Moses was cognizant of the dream and the promise. As he viewed the scene stretching out before him, maybe he recalled the calloused hands and the face of the old slave as he struggled to lift a large stone block and the relentless taskmasters as they drove the Hebrew slaves digging up mud, mixing it with straw, and endlessly toiling to build the pharaoh's monuments.

Perhaps he also recalled a time from his earlier days like the one depicted in *The Prince of Egypt*, the wild ride with Rameses in their chariots, racing through the marketplace, surfing the sand dunes, driving the horses to exhaustion. He might have smiled as he acknowledged the winner was always God! He had lived long enough to understand that God's seeming inaction did not mean He was incapable. It took a long journey for Moses to comprehend that he had to live by God's promises, not explanations.

14

The faithfulness of God in keeping His promises was apparent early in the life of this Hebrew prince of Egypt, born under the decree that every Israelite son be killed and cast into the river. The little ark fashioned by Moses' birth mother, Yocheved, and set afloat in the bulrushes to send him to safety and give him a chance to live became a vessel of redemption and mercy; it was constructed by faith, not coincidence. *The Prince of Egypt* reminds us in hair-raising fashion that the Nile River could be fraught with danger, full of crocodiles and hippopotamuses and other life-threatening perils. In an incredibly ironic twist, the very ruler who issued the decree took Moses into his court as a son. Pharaoh, whose compelling goal was to build his empire utilizing Hebrew slaves, was used by God in His faithfulness to nourish and rear Moses, the future deliverer of the Hebrews! What providence!

Although *The Prince of Egypt* does not emphasize these points, Moses, along with Rameses, would have acquired an outstanding education, been trained in military strategy, learned the art of charioteering, and more than likely soaked up anything the court retainers could teach him. This early learning experience was a prelude to being endowed with the wisdom of God and empowered to become a great leader.

LEADER OF THE SHEEP

The portrayal of Moses in Scripture and the film revealed a very human and vulnerable man. Born during one of the lowest points of Israel's history, he was chosen by God to lead the Israelites through crises. Nurtured in an excess of privilege throughout his early years, he experienced the burden of bondage when he was dispossessed and banished to the back side of the desert wilderness tending his father-in-law's flock of sheep—considered at the time to be a lowly, demeaning occupation. Forever encircled in God's sovereignty, Moses spent the most dynamic and dramatic years of his life after the God of the Bush confronted him.

Caring for sheep on a desolate desert plain was lonely and solitary work, which stood in stark contrast to the opulence of Moses' years as a member of Pharaoh's family in the powerful kingdom of Egypt. The desert provided endless hours to reflect, to wonder what twist of conscience had provoked him to attack and kill an overseer who was mercilessly beating an older Israelite slave—an act that caused Moses to flee for his life across the desert to the land of Midian. Although in *The Prince of Egypt* Rameses offers to "make it so it never happened" (POE), Moses cannot turn back. In that act he permanently forfeited his Egyptian identity and privilege and rejoined the people of his birth.

Leaving the palace was no doubt painful for Moses, not only giving up the lifestyle, but also being separated from friends and the only family he had ever known. We see this in *The Prince of Egypt* in the bittersweet exchange between Moses and his adoptive mother at the bathing pool where she found him when he was a baby. Moses' mistake of acting impulsively and taking things into his own hands puts flesh and blood on a Bible character. God's eventual response magnifies for us the infinite grace and inexhaustible patience of God—the very God who, according to the Bible, made a deposit of Himself in Moses' life. It was a deposit that became an irrevocable trust for the future. Moses is about to learn, in the later words of St. Augustine, that He loves each one of us as if there were only one of us.

16

THE GOD OF THE BUSH

According to the film, Moses' search for a lost sheep is diverted by an inexplicable event. A dry desert bush erupts into flames and then begins to blossom—an astonishing sight! It happens whenever the fire of God ignites and brings life. Hesitantly the puzzled shepherd approaches, extends his hand into the fire, and miraculously is not burned.

Moses, no longer wearing princely robes, in the heat of the Sinai Desert stands in the presence of God who appears to him in spite of his past, which included killing the Egyptian. He comes to Moses right where he is and calls him by name. The wilderness provides

Moses private time with God and is essential preparation for his public calling to the ultimate service. This training is meaningful and necessary as Moses encounters a faithful God keeping His promises. True, Moses killed an Egyptian, but God has endless deposits of mercy. The Bible records that mercy triumphs over judgment. When Moses feels abandoned, he discovers God on the side of mercy.

The Bible tells us that Moses turned aside to inspect a wondrous burning bush that was not consumed: "The Angel of the LORD appeared to him in a flame of fire from the midst of a bush. So he looked, and behold, the bush was burning with fire, but the bush was not consumed. Then Moses said, 'I will now turn aside and see this great sight, why the bush does not burn'" (Ex. 3:2–3 NKJV).

From the bush God spoke, "Moses, Moses!" God's act was all the more surprising because He had not revealed Himself or spoken audibly to Moses before. There was no prior warning or precedent in his life. Moses saw what God can do, even with those who may not be looking for Him in the desert places of life.

Moses answered God, saying, "Here I am," and God responded, "Do not draw near this place. Take your sandals off your feet, for the place where you stand is holy ground" (Ex. 3:5 NKJV).

Today we continue to be blessed by the surprise visits of God, the unexpected and unique times when we feel His presence. The visits may occur on the street corner, in the home, anyplace where God wants our attention. What is important is that we, like Moses, take the time to "turn aside" and willingly respond to the God of the Bush. He knows our names individually, our circumstances, and our conditions. God desires to be present in everyday life. Why? Because He is faithful in keeping His promises. He is aware of our very being, our wants, and our needs. He is always on the corner before we are there. Moses moved from slavery to faith and became a deliverer, and in so doing God kept His promise to Abraham.

For scores of years before Moses' birth, the people of Israel were in a fiery furnace of affliction in Egypt, yet they were not consumed. In speaking to Moses, God anointed a deliverer. Just as the bush was not consumed, the oppressed Israelites survived because "the LORD of hosts is with us; the God of Jacob is our refuge . . . God is our refuge and strength, *a very present* help in trouble" (Ps. 46:7, I NKJV, emphasis added).

Although God had been present in Moses' life from conception, in this incident He became "very present." Throughout Scripture we are reminded that God dwells within us; more than 366 times it is written that God is with us. I believe there is a difference between God as a present help and God as a very present help.

THE FAITHFULNESS OF GOD

Many pastors cross paths with people who are mentally disturbed. Such a man, recently released from jail, sent numerous death threats to me and eventually drove his car into the door of our church in an attempt to carry out his threats. I alerted the authorities, my ushers, and my staff. No one was harmed. I am convinced that what God says, He means. No weapon formed against us will prosper without God's permission (Isa. 54:17). The faithfulness He showed to the Israelites is the faithfulness we can hold on to today. He is in the midst of every battle. Believe me, during the crisis with the man who threatened me, God, though invisible, was a very present help. God does everything but fail.

19

In the Bible story, Shadrach, Meshach, and Abed-Nego were cast into a fiery furnace. Another being was sighted in the fire with them—a visible fourth person. It was God's angel of protection, and they were spared in His faithfulness to again show Himself strong. These are tests and lessons of trust, and such faith is rewarded.

We need to live in the conscious presence of God. Moses makes a mistake when he kills a man and honestly believes God will never give him another chance because of his sin. But as his sister, Miriam, points out to him in the film, he is a child of destiny, and it is ordained that he will be used to deliver his entire nation from oppression. God Himself comes to him in the bush, saying that He is not only present, but is very present. So present, in fact, that He tells Moses, "Where you stand is holy ground" (Ex. 3:5 NKJV).

In October of 1997, I experienced the faithfulness of God as never before—literally His very presence. I was seeking an innovative method to raise money for the Dream Center, the Los Angeles

International Church that my son, Matthew, copastors with me. I have pastored great churches that have experienced explosive growth, but the opportunity to serve in an inner city was elusive.

Sometimes referred to as a millennial city, Los Angeles is often out on the edge, a place connected by diversity. It comprises a frequently confusing American mosaic of cultures. In establishing our ministry there we had experienced a "burning bush" in our hearts. God was present and became very present. More than once, we have figuratively taken off our shoes in that ghetto, knowing we were standing on reclaimed, holy ground.

To celebrate my sixtieth year, I decided to walk from Phoenix to Los Angeles in a fund-raising effort for the Dream Center. Moses would probably have felt at home in the desert terrain I crossed. I have never felt the presence of God in such a way as during those days. Many times there would not be a vehicle in sight for two or more hours, other than the car that accompanied me on my journey. At the edge of Death Valley, the quietness and solitude were overwhelming. No one was in sight, yet the invisible God encompassed my way. Separated from everything, I could hear, "Be still and know that I am God."

The waterless landscape seemed endless until one day, almost like a mirage on the horizon, a small lake appeared right in the desert! Invigorating, it was a picture of biblical streams in the wilderness. There was no interstate, nothing but stretches of desert.

The occasional song of desert birds, the flutter of passing wings, and the treasured presence of God made me feel as though I were moving through surround sound. His protecting presence was evident when an out-of-control car came rushing toward me and missed. To me, that was another example of the faithfulness of God in keeping His promises.

My mind was clear, feeling only strength while focusing on God and the next destination. Gary Blair, my traveling companion, had driven off on an errand, and there had not been another car for hours. I started believing I would fail; I was not going to make it to the end of the trip. Doubt welled up in my mind. What would the people who had pledged their dollars think?

Suddenly a pickup truck approached from behind. After following for some time and causing me some alarm, the driver pulled alongside and asked if I was all right. He also wondered where I was going.

When I told him I was walking to Los Angeles, he was convinced I was either kidding or crazy. The scenario was like something from a B movie—only two days out of Phoenix and being quizzed about my trip by a stranger. I explained the mission was to raise money for the Dream Center—a place for drug addicts and alcoholics and others who had experienced life's failures to come and learn to dream again.

With tears in his eyes, he said he needed to go to the Dream

Center, adding that he was an alcoholic and drug user. He indicated that the quickest way to Los Angeles was through a nearby reservation, and he offered to guide me. By that time, Gary had returned and joined him. It was also an opportunity to share God's love with this thirty-something man in such bondage to sin. In the next few minutes, while I walked and prayed, he was led to Christ right there in the heart and heat of the desert. As He had done with Moses, God sought out that man precisely where he was and in His foreknowledge brought us together.

After asking Jesus to come into his life, the man wondered whether he could be baptized because he had heard somewhere that was a good thing to do. All we had on hand for such a sacred service was a bottle of Evian water. We ordinarily do not baptize by sprinkling, yet I felt that it was appropriate as an act of faith and obedience. When the man was baptized, we stood on holy ground.

My aching, blistered feet and tired body were rejuvenated. Even as God met Moses in the desert, He met a needy man on a lonely, seldom-traveled road and gave me, His servant, a fresh glimpse of a burning bush! It was a sign to travel on, a sign that continued to point not just toward Los Angeles, but to the All-Powerful One and His reclamation program for ruined lives. Did my pain and my lame walk attract the attention of that driver and God? It was another surprise visit of God, displaying His faithfulness to His people and to those He wants to be part of His forever family.

After twenty days, I arrived in Los Angeles, having raised the needed funds. The desert now has new significance to me, and I wonder if Moses, as I now sometimes do, longed to return to the solitude he knew during those years of shepherding when the burden of the doubting, murmuring children of Israel became intolerable. My desert crossing provided time for contemplation on the hope of eternal life that God promised long ago. He who promised is faithful.

What the burning bush meant to Moses is what it means to us today: "This shall be a sign to you that I have sent you" (Ex. 3:12 NKJV).

"I Am That I Am"

All through life the believer encounters signs that may not be unquenchable fire but that point to Jesus. The signs are vivid reminders of who God is and what He wants to do for His own. He promised His faithfulness to all generations.

Another person's burning bush may be an encouragement, but it is secondhand revelation. God wants to meet you individually so that you can come to know a God so real He even allows you to doubt! The burning bush was firsthand revelation to Moses as it commissioned him to lead his people out of Egypt to be God's dwelling place in the wilderness and in the land of Canaan.

An awesome scene in the film *The Prince of Egypt* shows Moses trying to locate the "voice" that surrounds him while the bush burns. As the breeze intensifies, with understandable timidity he dares ask, "Who are You?" (POE).

God replies, "I am that I am" (POE).

There is wonderful significance in this title that God assigns to Himself. Throughout the Scripture God's titles have direct bearing on the varied needs of the people with whom He has a relationship. His gracious and all-sufficient titles are there to meet every necessity of His people, concentrated in "I am that I am."

Still living on the back side of the desert at the foot of Mount Horeb, Moses remains uncomfortable as he attempts to reason with God while still holding on to his past transgression. One would think Moses had already witnessed enough signs and wonders portraying the divine presence of God. This is another example of a God who allows an individual to doubt. In perfect simplicity God uses what is available—the rod in his hand, the weakest of instruments familiar to the shepherd—to accomplish His sovereign goal. Excuses are erased. Moses is to allow God to take his nothingness and link it to Almightiness. How? Through the singular One who could make the statement "I am that I am."

> Fear not, for *I am* with you;
> Be not dismayed, for *I am* your God.
> I will strengthen you,
> Yes, I will help you,

I will uphold you with My righteous right hand.
(Isa. 41:10 NKJV, emphasis added)

Moses was aware of the very presence of God and His "righteous right hand," because it was a Hebrew expression. Commentaries point out that the character and personality of God in relation to His people are demonstrated through His right hand. The Jehovah name of God, which means "I am who I am," reveals what God wants to be to us. When He speaks of what He wants to do for His people, the right hand of God becomes significant. The "right hand" gives salvation, strength, action.

Long before, in His faithfulness, He promised to give the land of Canaan to the children of Abraham, Isaac, and Jacob. The burning bush was a symbol of God's promise of deliverance just as the rainbow was in the time of Noah. God remembers His promises. Delay is not denial: "All the promises of God in Him are Yes, and in Him Amen" (2 Cor. 1:20 NKJV).

God's patient affirmation in the film—"Oh, Moses, I shall be with you when you go"(POE)—is a gentle put-down to Moses. Even as the wind subsides and the fire fades before his eyes, he stands up, a new man. The God of the Bush is now within him.

Equipped with the eternal purpose of God and cognizant of His promises, Moses is ready for the challenge before him. He has witnessed the ever-present God. The past has no future as Moses anticipates his next step. He moves in secure awareness that the task ahead of him will never be as great as the Power behind him. Deep in his heart he may have mused that God does not always call the qualified, but He qualifies the called who are willing to be led by His righteous right hand.

THE FAVOR OF GOD

God was building a platform under the faith of Moses, and He seeks to do the same for us. This story is a mirror in which we can see our faithlessness or unworthiness revealed. Where have we missed the God of the Bush in our Christian walk? Have we been unwilling to take the time to "turn aside" as Moses did and see the sign that might not have been so dramatic? The God of the Bush is our God. Only twice in Scripture is that name equated with God. Once in the story of the burning bush and, again, so eloquently in Deuteronomy 33:16 (NKJV): "With the precious things of the earth and its fullness, and the favor of Him who dwelt in the bush." Many historic writers and researchers add the name "God of the Bush" to the other Jehovah names of God. Centuries later, the name remains important.

The favor noted in Deuteronomy 33:16 is often misconstrued. It was based on the suffering of Moses. Within that suffering, he learned what constituted genuine favor, and it became an indestructible foundation for his future. The promise of God's favor in the

Old Testament is valid for us today, but faith and obedience remain synonymous. This available favor is one of the capstones of God's blessing. The reference is made through Moses to Joseph and the promises to the faithful are activated because "not a word failed of any good thing which the LORD had spoken to the house of Israel. All came to pass" (Josh. 21:45 NKJV). Consider other references to His favor:

> For You, O LORD, will bless the righteous;
> With favor You will surround him as with a shield.
> (Ps. 5:12 NKJV)

> His anger is but for a moment,
> His favor is for life;
> Weeping may endure for a night,
> But joy comes in the morning . . .
> LORD, by Your favor You have made my mountain stand
> strong. (Ps. 30:5, 7 NKJV)

> For You are the glory of their strength,
> And in Your favor our horn is exalted. (Ps. 89:17 NKJV)

Jehovah God, the God of the Bush, waits to outpour His favor—literally His nature—on those who claim the promise. Incredible as it seems, to our faithlessness, He delights in showing Himself faithful!

A Modern-Day Servant of God

In a contemporary illustration, there are some personal similarities between Moses' "back side of the desert" years and Jim Bakker's experience. Currently Jim serves as a servant of God at the Dream Center. A question we might well ask about Moses' character is, Could a man with a criminal record become one of God's faithful representatives, even a deliverer? The answer given in Scripture is yes. Moses became God's choice in spite of his mistake, and this crossed my mind when Jim was invited to speak at one of the services at the Dream Center. He protested that he didn't want to create bad press for the ministry. I reminded him that God had given Moses a second chance.

28

Jim served hard time. He will never defend himself, but he relates that the desperate darkness of the prison experience brought him face-to-face with the God of the Bush. Clinging to a Bible for most of his waking hours, even when he felt God had abandoned him, he came to recognize that he had built his faith on the perceived lavish blessings of God instead of on seeking God's favor. Within the terrors of prison—paired with noted criminals—he discovered the favor of God as a "shield," which came from diverse directions through the prayers of God's people and inmates who for no known reason became his bodyguards and protectors. Two rape attempts were thwarted through this miraculous shielding. God's faithfulness in protecting His children was again evident.

It was my joy to join the "valley walkers" in encouraging Jim to dream again. Lost hope was restored in hundreds of little things that reminded him that the God of the Bush was ever present even when he was a prisoner of his aloneness. He realized the trial of faith is more precious than gold that perishes. God's favor, although sometimes unseen, brought a shield, life, and knowledge that the mountain of His favor stands strong.

The "horn exalted" in Psalm 89 translates as a symbol of power, achievement, and success. Success was redefined in a recent incident at the Dream Center—the former Queen of Angels Hospital— where Jim resides in the former nuns' quarters. He relates,

> I live in the Dream Center with my son, in adjoining rooms. One evening about eleven o'clock there was a knock on the door. Two young pastors said they had fifteen-year-old George, a boy who was so distraught they did not know what to do. He was convinced there was no God. He had just discovered his father had died of AIDS. His mother had returned to her native country and he was now alone. They wanted me to talk to him.
>
> I never felt more inadequate. What do you say to such a grieving youngster? The news about his dad was more than he could comprehend or tolerate. There could not be a God who would let the only living person close to him die.

I put my arms around him and tried to comfort him, giving him the usual Scriptures used when comforting someone in bereavement. Finally, after a long hour, in desperation more than inspiration, I decided to tell him about myself.

30

Quietly and reflectively I told about having everything of this world—houses, cars, servants, a seventy-foot yacht, and three thousand employees—and one day losing it all. I was sent to prison. The most difficult thing was losing the one I loved most. My wife divorced me and married my best friend.

I told him that although everything was gone, that did not include Jesus. He remained. Hebrews 13:5 says that God will never leave or forsake His own.

Only after I told him about going through the valley of the shadow of death and at times losing the will to live did he look at me. He said, "Jim, if you can make it, I will make it too." And he hugged me. It was one of the first moments that I knew beyond a shadow of doubt, I had been introduced to the God of the Bush, and it is His favor that matters most.

The story of Moses is symbolic to never give up on our dreams but to rely on the faithfulness of God. We need to give up our own strength. We should take time to "turn aside" when we hear God's voice. Everyone needs a burning bush so that God can be revealed in victory and defeat, in blessing and suffering. God delights in bestowing His favor on His own. We are called to activate the promises incumbent on His faithfulness: a shield for protection, an energized life, a mountain to stand strong over the deepest valley, and achieving whatever He pleases—success.

The Ultimate Deliverer

Years passed and Moses' journey was nearly complete. In his final message to the people he led through the wilderness—and whose performance he often lamented—he grieved. Why was the parting of the Red Sea not enough to bolster their faith? Was making the bitter waters at Marah sweet not a sign of God's faithfulness—past, present, and future? How many signs would it take for the God of the Bush to prove He was the I AM who went before?

Moses, in his anger, struck the rock twice, violating God's instruction. For that disobedient act, he was denied entrance into the promised land. But God, in His mercy, allowed him to climb Mount Nebo and view it from a distance.

Was God's promise denied? No, only delayed. God in His faithfulness allowed Moses to enter the ultimate promised land, appearing with Elijah on the Mount of Transfiguration.

Moses was a remarkable man—a tower and a fortress. He wanted to know not just God, but the ways of the God of the Bush. He experienced the faithfulness of God to His people. His lessons are to be engraved on our hearts, so with honor, we diligently wear the stamp of the Master's authority and approval on our journey. The movie *The Prince of Egypt* underscores God's protection. The Bible likewise teaches that mankind is a slave to sin. Faith in God, as in Moses' experience, comes from hearing, believing, and acknowledging the ultimate Deliverer.

How blessed we are to be on this side of the Cross! To see that when the inspired Word of God related a man's history in the Old Testament, it was presented with all his failures and imperfections. But in the book of Hebrews, the writer inscribed only the God-given purpose of that man's life. He told us that Moses endured, seeing Him who is invisible, living as if He was ever present. What a challenge to attune our spirits toward God, with hearts sensitive to the needs of those around us, mining the depths of truth revealed to us. Grant that we possess the vision to see into the distances as God sees, the faith to believe, and the courage to accomplish what He requires.

Moses, God's messenger, is a living photograph of the faithfulness of God in keeping His promises. In him we observe how God used the desert experiences to refine the Prince of Egypt. When our perceived strengths and weaknesses are exposed, we stand in humility before God, and the Prince of Peace stands ready to perform His best work in us. The future is as bright as the promises of God when our trust is in Him!

THE
DAY ON WHICH A
WORLD TURNED

JACK HAYFORD

*Jack Hayford reflects on the
mysterious fact that, as Moses discovered,
we do not know in advance the day
on which our world will turn.
On that glorious day, God will reveal
His purpose to us and release
our possibilities.*

The
Day on Which a
World Turned

he dawn is wakening. The bridegroom we saw the
night before lifts his head, gently leans over his yet-
sleeping love, lightly kisses her, and quietly rises to
leave their tent. But we realize *The Prince of Egypt* has
traversed more than the night following his wed-
ding. The once-but-no-longer-prince, now exiled to these desert sur-
roundings, is on the brink of a surprising new juncture in his life;
the screenplay has scrolled us directly from Moses and Tzipporah's
wedding to a sunrise—but not the one we thought.

Suddenly we are swept from the immediate to the transcendent.

A glance at Moses' aging features tells us that decades have
passed, and within moments we will discover—even more wonder-
ingly—this is *the* day of this man's life. It is the day on which a world
will turn—the day this man encounters his destiny, and the day a
nation takes its first step toward freedom.

Moses had awakened the same way for a thousand mornings.
Whether it was to deep blue crystal skies inset by the morning star
or to the whistling of the *hamsin* wafting its heated winds laden with

billions of minute sand grains that crept into every tent corner and crease. Whether his eyes opened to study Tzipporah's beauty on the pillow beside him, or he lifted his head from a rock on his hillside bed to scan the flock beneath his shepherd's watch point, he always rose to the same subtle internal accusation: *You've doomed yourself to a life in the desert.*

36

The thought was not the whimper of a self-pitying complaint; he was not a man to whine. Nor was it whispered within the soul of a man whose life held no pleasure at all. Rather, the idea stood starkly against the backdrop of a memory—the relentless images that constituted thoughts of *what might have been.*

As far as his earliest memories were informed, Moses had been born to wealth, splendor, and high promise. He was raised in the pharaoh's household, groomed for leadership in the atmosphere of the throne room of the world's grandest empire; the *might have been* of his past was as glorious as unlimited resources or unmatched power royalty could offer. But that wasn't the *might have been* that so often preoccupied his desert musings. No, Moses' constant raking of his soul was not over feelings of lost privilege, power, or prosperity. It was over the haunting sense of lost purpose.

Now—and for decades since his discovery—Moses was fully aware that his actual origins were not the same as his earliest recollections suggested. He had not been born to royalty, but had been adopted to it; he was found by the king's daughter (wife, as the film has it) to a moment of action that sought to serve his *life's purpose.* "*My peo-ple and yours!*" the voice seemed to thunder inside him.

A Life Turn into the Desert

Now it is all in the past. He is living in the seemingly endless con-sequence of one moment's quest to serve a blurred-but-present sense of duty (or is it purpose?). What had seemed to be his life had taken a screeching turn into the desert. And on this morning, Moses is up, but moving slowly.

He dislikes departure days. A long embrace will assure Tzipporah of his regret, leaving for springtime's pasturing season with her father's flocks. And on this morning, with a mind muddled by life's questions of meaning and his heart assessing the loneliness of the weeks ahead, Moses is about to step fully paced into the life that was always planned for him. He doesn't know it yet. He can't imagine it, not in his wildest dreams. But the world is about to turn in the glow of a bush.

Anyone else living here? There are few who never muse on a freeze-framed existence in their own private desert, just as Moses' soul is probed by questions: *Is my life God-deserted? Did my distant haste or folly permanently remove my highest possibilities? Is my purpose for being a closed book—its plot ruined by my blinded efforts at fulfilling it?*

Anyone else at this intersection—meeting himself in Moses' dilemma?

The question's answer is obvious: absolutely yes! We all have seasons of the soul when questions of life purpose haunt us. Every one of us has wondered at some point in life, *Will the day ever come? The day of a second chance, of renewed hope?* For Moses, the day has come, and the answer to these questions will be his before sunset.

That's the purpose of the story's telling.

The Prince of Egypt retells Moses' story to entertain us, and entertain us it does. But it is a film-story based on a fact-story, filled with a multitude of messages—every one of them loaded with hope! This theme of hope is at the heart of the Bible's whole message, whispering in the silence, shouting across history: there is a God, and His relentless love is seeking each of us! He comes to us in the desert places of the soul to announce His offer of grace and recovery of purpose for our lives: "I know the thoughts that I think toward you, says the LORD, thoughts of peace and not of evil, to give you a future and a hope" (Jer. 29:11 NKJV).

The same theme is echoed in the lyrics of the song "Through Heaven's Eyes," which Jethro sings in response to Moses' embarrassed retort upon finding a dinner served in his honor: "I have done nothing in my life worth honoring" (POE). In answer to the young man's despair, the High Priest of Midian delivers a message in music. It is set against a visual backdrop of Moses' life proceeding through desert years, but we will shortly discover that process is irresistibly flowing toward *the day on which a world turned*. The melody's heartbeat resounds with the Bible's hope-filled message: God has invested great worth in every person, and His plans of redeeming grace are to assure the possibility of recovering whatever has been lost!

Should a man lose ev'rything he owns
Has he truly lost his worth?
Or is it the beginning
Of a new and brighter birth?

So how do you measure the worth of a man?
In wealth or strength or size?
In how much he gained or how much he gave?
The answer will come,
The answer will come to him who tries
To look at his life through heaven's eyes.

A single thread in a tapestry,
Though its color brightly shine,
Can never see its purpose
In the pattern of the grand design . . .
So how can you see what your life is worth,
Or where your value lies?
You can never see through the eyes of man,
You must look at your life—
Look at your life through heaven's eyes! (POE)

God's purpose and value are written into the DNA of every soul, even if He and they are all denied. Still, He seeks us, and as with Moses, so it is with us all—God's quest to redeem, recover, and refocus is never for our own sake alone. There are always others whose destiny will be transformed if we allow Him to encounter and direct us. The call to "look at your life through heaven's eyes" is tuned to the same Voice that says, "Come to Me... and I will give you rest" (Matt. 11:28 NKJV).

42

Rest. It's a word well crafted to describe the fulfilling satisfaction of any of us who find God's hand retargeting our lives to find His best purposes for us. That *rest* is the term that describes the relief from whatever pointless or selfish wanderings have wearied our souls. When we enter it, in answer to God's redeeming promise, the beauty of what follows will spread beyond us to those we've been created to influence with His life, His love, and His hope. Moses' sensed call to liberate his enslaved people has a counterpart in ours. No one lives or dies to himself; there are others whose fulfillment will be realized only when we return from our own desert.

So the desert part of Moses' life, and the divine encounter he finds there, is a specific revelation. Don't make the mistake of saying of this film, "Hey, it's only a movie!" No, it portrays for us a pointed and personal unveiling of God's commitment to His purpose in people. It is a graphic lesson in the eternal fact that there are no deserts where God will leave us deserted. Our Creator is more than a distant deity; He is God-present-with-us! He is the One whose nature is to meet us at life's dark, dry, or desolate places; to forgive us at life's points of failure, compromise, or sin; and to point us back to His inimitable way for our lives.

He is the One who transforms the barren places, making it clear that they are places of His purpose designed to bring us to ours. They are "undeserted deserts"; locations in time and circumstance that, however seemingly empty of meaning, are about to become the place—the day—God comes to call us back to His high purpose. In *The Prince of Egypt*'s rendition of this timeless truth, Moses is again shown as a classic study of how magnificently the apparently "deserted life" can suddenly come to full fruition!

EVEN DESERTS ARE VISITED—AND BLOSSOM! Remember that fact when you wake up to another day in the desert. As it happened with Moses, there is never any way to recognize the morning of the day that your world will turn.

With the chiming of a wayward sheep's collar bell, the movie ushers us to the Bible's disclosure of a man's moment of truth. The words of Scripture not only emphasize that this dramatic moment is in one of the most improbable places, but subtly focus our attention on the faithfulness of a man to his duty: "And he led the flock to the back of the desert" (Ex. 3:1 NKJV). There is something to be said for "hanging in there," even when it seems we have been hung up. And there is an additional feature of the historical record, one obvious from a theological perspective but too often overlooked from the human. It's evident that Moses is distanced from his destiny's realization, both in time (years have passed) and in space (Egypt is a world away). But catch the point intended to be wedged into our minds: God knows where he is!

God never loses anyone's address.

"Of course. Obviously! So what?" Our human inclination is to presume that unless the brilliance of our intellect leads to the discovery, even the grandest truths are unworthy of our wonder. Possibly the wonder of this reality may too easily be discussed as inconsequential. "Sure! Any logical definition of *God* presumes absolute omniscience. If He exists, He knows everything." Don't miss the wonder of it. We can conclude that

God knows every person's name,

He knows everyone's thoughts,

He knows exactly where each of us is—at any moment;

geographically, where we are;

emotionally, how we're feeling;

intellectually, what we're thinking.

He knows the balance in our checkbooks,

the weariness in our bodies,

the anxiety in our hearts, and

any darkness shadowing our souls.

The Prince of Egypt is about to hear his own name uttered by the almighty Creator of mankind's millions. His address is known, and his name is spoken, seeming to echo off the walls of the canyons surrounding him: "Moses . . . Moses" (POE). In the middle of this moment, as a man draws near to examine a phenomenon beyond his natural explanation, the *personal* approach being made by a *personal* God summons our meditation on the depth of its meaning.

45

We are not exploring myth; we are studying history. All this is not simply a matter of human invention or pretentious presumption. God has revealed this to us, not only in Moses' story, but in express statements He has made in His Word. Psalm 139 sings the beauty of this truth:

> How precious also are Your thoughts to me, O God!
> How great is the sum of them!
> If I should count them, they would be more in number
> than the sand;
> When I awake, I am still with You. (vv. 17–18 NKJV)

To read the whole of the psalmist's poem is to hear God, as the eternal Father, described in the distinct sensitivity He feels for each of us and the detailed concerns He attends to in our interest. It is made clear forever: God's knowing is not merely intellectual and academic; it is personal, caring, and concerned.

To open a Bible and read the whole of Psalm 139 is to see how mankind's Father actually observes

- when we sit down and when we stand up (v. 2).
- what we are thinking and where we are going (vv. 2–3).
- when we were conceived and how we entered life (vv. 13–15).
- how we would develop and when we would be born (v. 16).

The Prince of Egypt focuses this truth in Moses' burning bush encounter. That is the setting in which the film rehearses the confrontation Moses is shown to have had with his sister earlier. In the presence of God, he is brought to a flashback of her words as God's reminder of his union with this enslaved people: "You were born of my mother, Yocheved! You are our brother!" (POE). Though not a part of the biblical record, it unites Moses' heredity and his mission, and it reminds us of God's personal attentiveness to who we really are and what we are really about.

This is truth for our times. We are not cosmic accidents, but personal, created creatures planned by a personally caring Creator.

Jesus in the Sermon on the Mount reinforced the richness and reality of God's personal care for each of us. In a brilliantly tender series of statements, He emphasized our Father-Creator's vast ocean of love—showing how His care for the slightest creature verifies the abundance of His care available for each of us. He declared mankind to be His most noble creation:

> Do not worry about your life . . . Look at the birds of the
> air, for they neither sow nor reap nor gather into barns; yet
> your heavenly Father feeds them. Are you not of more
> value than they? Which of you by worrying can add one
> cubit to his stature? So why do you worry about clothing?
> Consider the lilies of the field, how they grow: they neither
> toil nor spin; and yet I say to you that even Solomon in all
> his glory was not arrayed like one of these. Now if God so
> clothes the grass of the field . . . will He not much more
> clothe you, O you of little faith? Therefore do not worry...
> For your heavenly Father knows that you need all these
> things. But seek first the kingdom of God and His righ-
> teousness, and all these things shall be added to you. (Matt.
> 6:25–33 NKJV)

47

By every means possible, God reveals His constancy of concern
for even the minor details of our lives (Luke 12:6–7). We are also
reminded that His love gifts of life and forgiveness carry with them
the guarantee of our welcomed access into His presence—seeing
He is sympathetic with our weaknesses (Heb. 4:14–16) when in
straits of struggle, when in times of trouble, when weary with life's
warfare.

But it's hard to remember all this during a long desert sojourn.

Our deserts have a way of burning out these thoughts. Our arguments born of the tough desert realities we face stand in contrast with the larger truth of God's unfailing presence. But irrespective of how distant or dry our back side of the desert may be, it is never outside the circle of God's loving attention or the scope of His power and His readiness to act. There will always come an appointed moment when His approach will indicate His personal care, and at that time—however late it may seem to us—He will make another awe-inspiring truth dramatically clear.

A TRIPLE-POINTED MESSAGE

Few Bible episodes are better known. The burning bush is more than merely miraculous; the event contains a triple-pointed message for us all, summarized in five words: *God's intended purpose is indestructible.*

God not only gained Moses' attention through the phenomenal demonstration of the burning bush, but He also made a statement about the indestructible nature of His purposes. The fact that the bush was aflame but remained unconsumed holds a dramatic insight: the unquenchable fire of God's presence and purpose renders its bearer indestructible while that purpose is still alive!

Moses witnessed a message that answered his inner questionings of lost purpose. The message is the same to you and me. The hopes and dreams heaven has put in our hearts are not flimsy. However burned out our desert may have caused us to feel, God's

purposes for and in us are indestructible facts. Our frailty is no lim-
itation to the durability of the flame of His purpose. Once His
eternal purpose enflames our souls, the fragility of our humanness
or our fallibility in circumstances will never bring the flame to
naught if we will come, stand, and live in His presence. So it was
that God said, "Take the shoes from off your feet, for the place on
which you stand is holy ground" (POE).

49

A first impression, whether witnessing *The Prince of Egypt* or reading the same words in the Bible, is to draw a common conclusion—
that God's command was "religious," simply a call to strike a pious
pose. But however distant in history this religious practice may
reach, the call moved well beyond mere piety of performance. God
is not into religious calisthenics, but He does have practical, physical ways of making spiritual trust real to us.

There are a divine logistic and a divine logic in this command.
The *logistic* has to do with something only God is able to supply; the
logic is seen in the sensible "steps" He directs so that "supply" can
be received. Moses is being called to "step" into a new realm of possibility—into a quality of life he cannot produce on his own.

What is "holy ground"? And why is it important to "stand"
there? Simply stated, it is turf that has come under the touch of
God, and it cannot be produced by human actions. Only God can
make anything holy. We have a human habit of designating religious
personalities as holy men, and that is not necessarily bad. But it leads

to the impression that such people—and Moses surely became one—have arrived at that designation by reason of their devotion rather than by the grace of God's deliverance.

Deliverance is a good word; it's another word for *salvation,* the most beautiful word the Bible uses to describe how God meets me at where and as what I'm not in order to bring me to where and *unto what* He intended! So God was inviting Moses to commit to the fundamental fact of every human life: to stand up with God, I must come to Him on the terms of His holiness, not my own. To do otherwise is to exhibit human arrogance, and it is to ultimately arrive at a dead-end street of earth-time limitations and forever-time insufficiency.

In the light of the logistical fact of God's supplied resource for Moses' calling, the logic of God's Word, "take the shoes from off your feet," becomes all the more evident. To step out of his shoes was an action with clear implications: I step out of what I have produced into the possibilities that You have created. It is more than merely likely that in that nomadic world, Moses would have fashioned his own sandals. But in either case—self-made or, more broadly, man-made—the message is this: if the place you stand is the realm of your own creation, you will always remain limited to your own capacities. So come, taste, and test the potential of walking into My creative possibilities.

He didn't know the details yet, but Moses was about to be summoned to face a cluster of impossibilities forty years long

50

and a wilderness wide:

- An unyielding monarch
- An army in hot pursuit
- An ocean lying as an obstacle to escape
- A desert-journey with a million mouths to feed

And the beat goes on. Only a God with an infinitely larger degree of capability than man at his best can provide the assistance that Moses would need or that we will.

The call to become barefoot in the presence of God is an eloquent summons to honesty. It called Moses to a declaration of dependence upon the Almighty, and it calls us to the same declaration. There is a divine quest today as then, a call for more than one man named Moses, a call for a barefoot battalion of honest souls that will be open to what God is able to do *in* their lives and *through* them.

For the fullest majesty of His mightiness to become manifest through any of us, one thing remains—and Moses found it.

FEELING GOD'S HEART...PACED BY HIS HEARTBEAT

The Prince of Egypt is a refreshing piece from Hollywood—a lovely evidence that our fabled Tinsel Town can produce something as ennobling and spiritually enriching as it is entertaining and economically successful. We applaud such enterprise! It is a mix of the biblically factual and the humanly imaginative. It brings us scenes that

- demonstrate the wrongness of human-to-human cruelty and injustice.
- stir our delight in brotherly camaraderie and romantic mystery.
- quicken our sense of spiritual inquiry and longing for meaningful destiny.
- salt and pepper it all with comic relief and colorful artistry.

But within the story a tender thread is woven of yet another quality: the divine grace of compassion as it is awakened in a human spirit, and God's timeless call to action as that grace is amplified in us.

From the film's opening snap of a whiplash, as the clouds of earth shift and roil, to the sometime sounds of earth's pain contrasted with our sometimes glimpse of sunlight in heaven; from the wild, madcap chariot race of two youthful princes in an ancient court to the time one of them becomes captivated with the captives, moved from indifference to indignation over the plight of the oppressed; from the tender lullaby of a slave mother forced to surrender her child to the plaintively groaned lyric of "with the sting of the whip on my shoulder, with the salt of the sweat on my brow" (POE), a value is being highlighted: *compassion*. That awakens *concern*. That prompts *action*.

52

The Prince of Egypt is not a "message" film, but it is a film with a message at its heart. And it couldn't really be any other way because it is derived from the Word of God. It is a dramatic account of such historic and redemptive dimensions, it cannot escape sowing certain seeds of truth in those who will listen and look. We can be thankful it is being screened, but it is most important that it be seen with the eyes of the heart.

53

The story of Israel's slavery in Egypt,
The revelation of God's heart of agony over their pain,
The summons of God to call and capacitate a deliverer—
These reveal God's heart.

The record of God's miracles of power,
The numerous offers of divine mercy if Pharaoh would yield,
The salvation God gave through the Passover lamb—
These reveal God's heart.

But also note,

The determination of a boy to forsake status
and convenience,
The indignation of a privileged prince over the
inequity and injustice surrounding him,
The refusal of a man to deny his identity
though it disadvantaged him—
These reveal God's heart overtaking a person.

And finally note,

> The discovery of a man who missed his first chance
> that there was a God who hadn't forgotten him,
> The surprise of a man who found his second chance
> could be found at the feet of God,
> The surrender of a man who stepped out of fear and
> uncertainty to serve God's will in caring for others—
> These reveal God's heart possessing a person,
> bringing him beyond feeling God's heart
> to being paced by His heartbeat.

54

It is not outside the realm of reason to believe the same God who met Moses in his desert is whispering to us through this ancient Prince of Egypt to draw us to higher purposes than we know. His actions there and then speak forever into our here and now. By them, God has revealed the reality that no human desert of apparent pointlessness or difficulty is ever deserted by Him; and that no one need live without the hope that God's love invites you to let Him make today the day on which your world turns.

There is a world of human hearts enslaved by a heartless inhumane world—waiting for someone. To answer that heart cry, the same God who called and sent Moses is still meeting people as uncertain of themselves as Moses was, revealing His purpose to them and releasing their possibilities through His love, His power, and His grace.

Coming to stand on God's holy ground, these become equipped as His barefoot battalion. They are the freed and forgiven few who find their highest dreams fulfilled as they surrender in faith to the Giver of dreams—our Creator-Father, who has become our Redeemer-Lord.

He is the One Moses discovered at a bush, the day the Prince of Egypt found the Light that brought his life's dawning. And he is the same One to whom *The Prince of Egypt* points us if we would discover ours.

55

WE SAY "NO"...
GOD SAYS
"YES!"

JONI EARECKSON
TADA

Moses' story shows that
God often chooses the most unlikely people
to accomplish His will. Joni Eareckson Tada
relates her life's experience to God's use
of human weakness—physical or otherwise—
for His glory.

WE SAY "NO"...
GOD SAYS "YES!"

hat do you expect from me, the *impossible?*"

You've said it. I've said it. And Moses said it. Thing is, with Moses, God was indeed asking the impossible. And from a bush at that. A flaming bush. With branches unscathed. Impossible! The voice of God spoke from the furnace, presenting Moses with an absurd mission: "I have come down to deliver them out of slavery and bring them to their promised land . . . And so unto Pharaoh I shall send you" (POE).

It was unthinkable, laughable, yes, impossible. *Me, Moses, I'm supposed to round up a couple of million people or so—people in bondage, who know nothing but bricks and straw, who haven't a clue about packing up and heading anywhere other than the stone quarries, people who think the earth stops beyond the Red Sea—and tell them God has commanded me to lead them out of Egypt and into a land flowing with milk and honey?*

Against the corner of the canyon wall, standing in the presence of the Lord God, Moses proceeds to argue, listing one "no" after the other. The list is in the book of Exodus, and it's echoed in these

59

lines from *The Prince of Egypt:* "Me? Who am I to lead these people? They'll never believe me. They won't even listen!" (POE).

Any realist would have agreed. Any straight-thinking, straw-stomping, brick-laying Hebrew would laugh and say, "The Lord would do better to give us a real leader, a *man* at least, someone with strength and courage; not this weather-worn shepherd from the back side of the desert who's not even willing to take on the job!"

Moses lists more "noes." Not only will the people refuse to listen to him, but they will refuse to listen to God. He can just picture the Hebrew slaves laughing at him, saying, "We haven't heard from God in centuries. Miracles haven't happened in millennia. How do we know God is strong enough? We're not convinced He can deliver on His promises! Not only this, if God were God, He'd *never* choose the son of the man who slaughtered our children."

In the Exodus account, Moses had one final "no." He threw in the face of God his dysfunctional "adult son of adoptive parents" speech: "I've had a bad childhood . . . I'm a stutterer . . . a poor speaker. To be honest, I'm just plain *handicapped!*"

AN IMPOSSIBLE DREAM

"I'm just plain *handicapped!*" I'm not a Moses, but I can identify with prophets who argue with God about impossibilities. After I broke my neck in a 1967 diving accident in which I became a quadriplegic, He asked the impossible of me. Lying paralyzed on a hospital bed, staring straight up at the ceiling, I seemed to hear the voice of God, saying, *Joni, I want you to live life without use of your hands or legs and learn to smile while doing it.*

"Lord," I said as I laughed and shook my head, "that's impossible!"

What's more, God seemed to be saying, *I want you to be My audio-visual aid of how My strength shows up best in weakness.*

"*What?* People won't believe in me. They'll say, 'If her legs are paralyzed, her brain must be too. Anybody who's *that* dependent can't be very self-directed, can't accomplish much.' People won't believe You, either, God. It'll be, 'How can God be good if He would allow something like permanent paralysis to happen to her? God must not be very caring or compassionate.'"

God persisted. Maybe His voice didn't boom from a burning bush, but I could hear Him speak in hushed, soft tones in the middle of dark, lonely nights in the hospital. On one of those dark nights I finally got to the crux of the issue. Like Moses, I wasn't so much concerned about people believing in me or people believing in God. The fact was, I didn't believe in myself: "I can't do anything, not even peel an orange or walk across a room. What good am I to myself? To anybody?" Insecure and unsure, seething with doubts and resentments—that was me. That was Moses.

God had an answer for me. It was the same as His answer to Moses. The Lord almighty said it in Exodus 4:11, and it is echoed in one of the most dramatic scenes in *The Prince of Egypt*. In the film,

61

the light from the burning bush seems to burn the canyon walls, wrapping Moses in an intense, incandescent glow. The voice of God is tinged with anger. He has something to say about the subject of handicaps. He booms, "Who made man's mouth? Who made the deaf, the mute, the seeing, or the blind? Did not I? Now go!" (POE).

SINNERS IN THE HANDS OF AN ANGRY GOD

It's a testy thing to go up against the God of the universe. To provoke the Almighty. To disagree with destiny. It's one thing to say, "God, are You sure You have the right person?" and another to say, "God, You have the wrong person!"

That's pretty much the tack Moses took. *The Prince of Egypt* doesn't have the time to elaborate, but the biblical account lingered on this scene. Moses refused God altogether, saying in Exodus 4:13, "Lord, please! Send someone else" (TLB). After all the appealing, cajoling, discussing, and arguing, he broke off negotiations with God.

I pretty much did the same. I thought, *Surely, God, You've got the wrong person. I can't be Your audiovisual aid of how Your strength shows up best in weakness. Find somebody who was born with a disability. Get somebody who's a veteran at this. A rehab professional. Miss Wheelchair America. But not me.*

"No, God, I won't!" We say it in countless small and subtle ways when we sense the Lord is asking the impossible of us. "Not me!"

Stop and consider the foolishness of saying "no" to God. It's unthinkable, laughable, yes, impossible. The nerve of puny Joni. How dare Moses! Who do they think they're dealing with? The God they have refused—the God so many of us dig in our heels against—this God sets billions of stars spinning in motion; commands animals to hibernate; sustains birds on the wing; holds protons and neutrons together in atoms; keeps planets in line, gravity pulling, water evaporating, trade winds blowing, plants photosynthesizing, worms burrowing, cows lactating, electronic forces repelling and attracting, sperm and eggs connecting, blood flowing, quasars pulsating, low and high pressure areas balancing, galaxies circling, and the sky from falling. *How can mere man refuse God? The audacity!*

63

God is righteous; we're not. He's holy and we're haughty. He's pure and we're proud. He owns everything and we're just renting space and borrowing time.

So what does God do? Consider the poignant scene in *The Prince of Egypt* that depicts God's response, His gracious nature in the face of our stubbornness. Moses cowers against the canyon wall. He's too afraid to look into the light of the burning bush. Because He knows Moses' fear, God's anger subsides. God reaches out with the wind and the light of the bush to gently embrace and comfort Moses. Moses is lifted up and brought closer to the bush. God assures His servant: "Oh, Moses, I shall be with you when you go to the king of Egypt" (POE).

Artistically the illustrators of *The Prince of Egypt* paint a beautiful picture of this scene in soft tones and gentle shadows. We learn that

God is not even angered when we say "no"—at least not for long. God is not worried, unsure, petty, or caught off guard. He doesn't bite His nails, blow His stack, overreact, or make heads roll just because we say no. He's not a threatened, pacing deity starving for attention, but the blessed, that is, happy, Ruler who alone is immortal. Good thing for Moses.

Good thing for me. Listen to how the Bible depicts it:

> He revealed his will and nature to Moses and the people of Israel. He is merciful and tender toward those who don't deserve it; he is slow to get angry and full of kindness and love. He never bears a grudge, nor remains angry forever. He has not punished us as we deserve for all our sins, for his mercy toward those who fear and honor him is as great as the height of the heavens above the earth. He has removed our sins as far away from us as the east is from the west. He is like a father to us, tender and sympathetic to those who reverence him. For he knows we are but dust and that our days are few and brief, like grass, like flowers, blown by the wind and gone forever. But the lovingkindness of the Lord is from everlasting to everlasting, to those who reverence him; his salvation is to children's children of those who are faithful to his covenant and remember to obey him! (Ps. 103:7–18 TLB)

What a God! That the burning bush did not explode and consume Moses, reducing him to ashes, is incredible. That God did not snuff me out in a nanosecond, even as I rammed my wheelchair against my parents' living room wall in stubborn defiance, is incredible. Who are we, the creatures, to tell God "no"? The Lord could have turned the burning bush into a welding torch, focusing His white-hot wrath in our direction. Justice would have demanded it. But the nature of God is to be not only just, but also merciful. James said that mercy triumphs over justice (2:13).

65

God, however, went one better than mercy. He showed *grace*.

GOD WON'T TAKE "NO" FOR AN ANSWER

To teach the deeper lesson, let's go to the deeper source, the Bible. Because *The Prince of Egypt* could fully develop only a limited number of characters, the filmmakers cast Aaron, the brother of Moses, the first high priest of the Hebrew nation, differently from the way he's portrayed in Exodus. So we'll follow the scriptural record at this juncture. It'll help make clear exactly why God won't take "no" for an answer.

We've already seen that God did not vent His anger at Moses' break-off of negotiations. Rather, He showed mercy. But it was a *severe* mercy: God didn't snuff him out; He just made things more difficult for Moses. God teamed Moses up with his brother, Aaron. Exodus 4:14–16 (TLB) describes it this way:

Then the Lord became angry. "All right," he said, "your brother Aaron is a good speaker. And he is coming here to look for you, and will be very happy when he finds you. So I will tell you what to tell him, and I will help both of you to speak well, and I will tell you what to do. He will be your spokesman to the people. And you will be as God to him, telling him what to say."

Yes, Moses was spared, but, no, things wouldn't get easier. It would be a *hard* mercy. God fulfilled His purpose by way of this curious team of Moses and Aaron, a poor shepherd and, as the Bible depicts Aaron, an aging priest—God's prophet was given a second prophet and God's proxy, another proxy of His own. It was no longer the original plan of God speaking to Moses speaking to Pharaoh. It was now God speaking to Moses who translated the message to Aaron who then communicated it all to the king of Egypt. The series of mediations between God and man became longer than was originally envisioned. How many sources of error were there in the transmission from mouth to mouth with a slow tongue?

It's the story of what happens when stubborn people say no to God. I can identify. Sure, God was merciful to me in that, in my weakness and resentment, He didn't give up on me. I didn't die from some weird lung infection or perish on the operating table. Thank heavens for that!

Nevertheless, even though I lived, living was not easy. Thinking about the similarities between the clumsy, time-consuming plan involving Aaron the Extra and my own situation, I wonder how many weeks and months of depression and boredom I could have bypassed had I agreed with God in the beginning? I spent so many of my early days in my wheelchair idling away time in front of a television, apathetic and self-pitying.

67

Stubbornness makes for long transactions between us and God.

It's amazing that God continues to work in the lives of stiff-necked, contrary people. More slowly, but He *does* work. He just won't take "no" for an answer. And that fact begins to shed light on another more amazing fact: *if God is heaven bent on using us—even when we resist Him—then He must have something extraordinary in mind. We must be destined to fit in a great and godly plan!*

Think of it. We are worth the effort. We are not easily discarded. We are people for whom God will go the third mile and the fourth mile. This is more than mercy! We can identify with a God who might force us to grovel in the dirt and crawl to Him to beg for mercy. A God like this we can relate to, we can understand (especially if we've made matters worse through our obstinacy).

But the God of the Bible isn't like this. Psalm 103:8 (TLB) suggests, "He is merciful and tender toward those who don't deserve it." He's the earnest Shepherd searching for the wayward sheep, running down the path looking for the lost lamb, urgent and passionate in pursuing the balky and bullheaded.

This is more than mercy, friend. This is where the *grace* comes in. When it begins to dawn, as it did on Moses, that we are the recipients of grace—that is, unexplainable, effervescent divine favor, happy-hearted, heaven-sent approval—you're gripped! When that "aha!" moment breaks over you and you realize that, although you deserve heaven's slap, you are feeling God's embrace, you are left speechless. Dumbstruck. Awestruck.

And you will never be the same. Neither was Moses. Jethro's song "Through Heaven's Eyes" from *The Prince of Egypt* portrays it beautifully:

> A lake of gold in the desert sand
> Is less than a cool, fresh spring
> And to one lost sheep, a shepherd boy
> Is greater than the richest king.
> Should a man lose ev'rything he owns,
> Has he truly lost his worth?
> Or is it the beginning
> Of a new and brighter birth?
>
> So how do you measure the worth of a man?
> In wealth or strength or size?
> In how much he gained or how much he gave?
> The answer will come,

The answer will come to him who tries

To look at his life through heaven's eyes.

So how do you judge what a man is worth?

By what he builds or buys?

You can never see with your eyes on earth.

Look through heaven's eyes.

Look at your life

Through heaven's eyes! (POE)

69

GOD IRRESISTIBLE

This is what God has been aiming at all along. This is why grace covers mercy, which triumphs over justice. God must make Himself inexorable to Moses. God must make Himself irresistible, undeniable, and irrefutable. To me, to us. And there is an astounding reason.

Moses couldn't figure it out at first. All he knew was that the Lord was determined to have His way in spite of all his objections. In *The Prince of Egypt,* there is a touching and powerful moment when Moses kneels before the bush—the wind subsides and the final light in the branches fades. The film shows Moses sitting in awed silence after God has had final say. Moses accepts this. He has fallen quiet. He looks at his staff lying on the ground near his leg. With a look of resolve, he takes up the staff.

God has prevailed. The arguing has ceased. The bargaining is over. Moses left the bush, now just an ordinary piece of desert shrub, and "took his wife and sons, put them on a donkey and started back to Egypt. And he took the staff of God in his hand" (Ex. 4:20 NIV).

God had won. Moses no longer called it "his staff"; it was "the staff of God." The stiff-necked attitude dissipated into quiet submission to an irresistible God. Moses *was* special, and he knew it—not in a proud and insolent way, but in humility. He was the wayward sheep, now found. He was the balky and bullheaded, now tamed. He was destined, so he stepped into his destiny and walked back into Egypt.

Friend, this is where change happens. This is why God asks the impossible, of Moses and of us. This is why the Lord, when He has set His designs on us, won't take "no" for an answer. This is why the Lord almighty sets aside His wrath and pursues us. This is also why He makes things more difficult—*God must make Himself irresistible in our eyes.* God must hear us echo the song of Moses in Exodus 15:11 (KJV): "Who is like unto thee, O LORD, among the gods? Who is like thee, glorious in holiness, fearful in praises, doing wonders?"

When we give way to the Force that is stronger than ourselves, greatness begins! When we come to the place where we realize we cannot resist our destiny, when our stubbornness is broken, when we, the wayward sheep, walk lowly next to the Shepherd, change happens; we then realize that everything we say and do depends on trust in the Lord alone. For Moses and for us, God becomes compelling. And we become relentless in pursuing Him. *As a result, Moses becomes ruthless toward himself and his people, and even more so toward the mighty Pharaoh.*

The emphatic "No!" has become a resounding "Yes!" It's no longer "not me"; it's "pick me!" The weakness has become strength, of cast iron. The frustrated plan has become more gloriously perfect. The tragedy has become triumphant. The coward has become ennobled. Everything wrong has turned out right, the *best* kind of right.

71

This resolve would be urgently needed as Moses went up against Pharaoh. There had to be no room for second-guessing. No self-doubts. Standing in front of the throne of the king of Egypt, harassed by the Hebrews, questioned by his family, assaulted by his enemies, Moses needed rock-solid determination, his heart unbreakable, his mind unyielding.

This is the astounding reason why God makes Himself irresistible. It is for our sakes. It is for the sake of advancing the kingdom.

This is the path I've wheeled down for more than thirty years in a wheelchair. I've left in the dust comments such as, "That's impossible!" and "Nobody will believe me!" I had once turned my back on God, insisting He find some other guinea pig to be His audiovisual aid of how God's strength shows up best in weakness. And like the minds of so many prophets and priests and people in the past, my mind was boggled by God's doggedness toward me, courting and chasing, pursuing and hounding until I was gripped.

THE IMPOSSIBLE DREAMS OF WEAK PEOPLE

The story of Moses is a story of God's power showing up best and most beautifully through weak people. Not just physically weak, but weak-minded. Weak-willed. Weak in the knees. It's like the "staff of Moses" becoming the "staff of God"—the staff was still a rough-hewn wooden pole cut from a tree, but as Moses lifted it up to God, it became a royal scepter of divine power. In the same way, God plucked Moses out of the desert, infusing his heart and energizing him to stand before the most powerful monarch in the world to pronounce unflinchingly, "Let my people go!" (POE). What clout! God used the weakness of Moses to reduce him to ashes so that a phoenix might rise from the ruins. That's the way God works.

In this wheelchair, I've learned a lot from Moses. I've learned that God delights in taking on stiff-necked, stubborn people. He delights in choosing the unlikely, ill-equipped, and untrained to get a job done. This is hard for most people to understand. Remember my reasoning, God, You've got the wrong person . . . Get somebody who's a veteran at this. A rehab professional. Miss *Wheelchair America.* It's the way we usually think.

Consider the job of leading millions of slaves out of Egypt. If we were God, how would we have gotten the job done? Most of us would have picked the smartest men and women this side of the Sinai Desert to be on our team. Our strategic planning sessions would have included the ancient equivalents of Ph.D.s and Madison

Avenue types. We would have sicced our best public relations people on to the job, advance men covering the palace grounds, holding focus groups among the pharaoh's guard. We would have sent out professional headhunters to find and employ the best speakers this side of the Delphi Oracle to state the case before the king of Egypt. Stumblers and bumblers? Not a chance. Stutterers? Never. Our man—the vision bearer—would be smooth in speech, skilled in tongue, and as good a debater as Aristotle himself. The whole operation would require departments and budgets. To qualify even as a mere rank-and-file member of our organization, an applicant would have to be smart, monied, gifted, young, athletic, and unusually attractive.

Weak people need not apply. Those with physical defects? Forget it. People who might slow down our progress? Never. A man or a woman whose life is filled with problems? A murderer on the run, like Moses? Not on your life. We would accept only the cream of the crop.

This is the way the world works. But thank God, we're not running the world. He is. And He opens His arms wide to people who are poor, sick, ugly, lonely, weak, ungifted, unlovely, and unlikely. God's great love mandates it. Plus what's in a person's heart matters more to Him than what's on the outside. God put it this way: "Don't judge by a man's face or height, for this is not the one. I don't make decisions the way you do! Men judge by outward appearance,

but I look at a man's thoughts and intentions" (I Sam. 16:7 TLB).
It's a good thing.

But there's another reason God relentlessly pursues people like
you—if you consider yourself weak—and me. Let's return for a
moment to the story of Moses.

Any struggle between a hero and the bad guys is interesting
enough in itself. An encounter between *any* leader of the Hebrews
and the king of Egypt would have been dramatic. But when the hero
is disadvantaged, a new element is introduced. The hero, if he is a
bumbler from the back side of the desert who smells like sheep, has
less chance of winning. The odds are against him. But if he over-
comes in spite of the odds, he ends up twice as much of a hero
because he wins through weakness.

All through the Bible God shows us that this is exactly the way
He does things to bring maximum glory to Himself. The Hebrew
slaves should have known this. They should have remembered the
story of their father, Abraham. God promised him a nation of
descendants as numerous as the stars in the heavens. But then He gave
Abraham a barren wife. *That's no way to start a nation of people,* we think.

The Bible includes other examples. Centuries after Moses, God
would send a teenage shepherd boy named David to do battle
against Goliath, the seasoned warrior giant of the Philistines. *That's
no way to slay an enemy,* we think. Then look what God did to Gideon.
He whittled Gideon's 32,000-man army down to a mere 300 before

74

sending them out to fight hoards of Midianites. *That's no way to win a war,* we think.

Why does God do things this way? So that when the Midianites were routed, Goliath had fallen, and Sarah had given birth to a beautiful baby boy, *the whole world would know that God, not man, had done it.*

In the New Testament, the apostle Paul made a theology out of it. He told the Corinthian Christians to look around at themselves and realize that, on the whole, God called people into their fellowship who, by human standards, were not wise, influential, or of noble birth. The apostle was saying that often God deliberately chooses weak and limited and unlikely candidates to get His work done so that when the job is accomplished, the glory goes to Him and not to us. Think of it! The very weakness and problems you and I find so painful are just what He uses to honor Himself. We are not a golden scepter in His hand. We are a shepherd's crook, picked off the dirt and fashioned into "the staff of God."

Again, this is simply the way God does things. Another prophet named Zerubbabel who followed in Moses' footsteps learned this. Zechariah 4:6–7 (TLB) states plainly, "'Not by might, nor by power, but by my Spirit, says the Lord of Hosts—you will succeed because of my Spirit, though you are few and weak.' Therefore no mountain, however high, can stand before Zerubbabel! For it will flatten out before him! And Zerubbabel will finish building this

75

Temple with mighty shouts of thanksgiving for God's mercy, declaring that all was done by grace alone."

There we are back to that word again: *grace*. "My grace is sufficient for you, for my power is made perfect in weakness." God said that in 2 Corinthians 12:9 (NIV). And I would echo the next line: "Therefore I will boast all the more gladly about my weaknesses, so that Christ's power may rest on me . . . I delight in weaknesses, in insults, in hardships, in persecutions, in difficulties. *For when I am weak, then I am strong*" (emphasis added).

76

I'm so grateful God reduced me to ashes in this wheelchair. In my weakness, I have learned, like Moses, to lean hard on God. The weaker I am, the harder I lean on Him. The harder I lean, the stronger I discover Him to be. The stronger I discover God to be, the more resolute I am in the job He's given me to do, and the more I realize that God simply will not empower a proud, self-sufficient vessel. It's little wonder I delight in difficulties. (I'm not choosing suffering; I'm just choosing God!)

Choosing God

I wonder what the Hebrew slaves thought when they first heard that God wanted to deliver them? Their idea of deliverance probably sounded like this: the same divine power that led Abraham, chose Isaac, and wrestled with Jacob, this great God of our forefathers will one day part the heavens and descend upon the evil forces at our camp gates. God will come like a king with great armies, trumpets, majesty, and splendor, and we will follow Him, striding gloriously into a new day! In your dreams.

The story of their deliverance is quite different. It is human, gutsy, earthy, and nonsentimental. In the Bible's portrayal, as well as in *The Prince of Egypt,* Moses is not touched up like a Michelangelo portrait. All of the prophet's ugly little weaknesses are showcased. Especially his most shameful: "No! Not me, God. Send somebody else!"

Yet the story of Moses is a story of justice, mercy, and *grace.* It's a story about freedom God's way. He does not free Hebrew slaves through powerful displays of conjured miracles so much as He frees them through ordinary, weak people. No Ph.D.s or Madison Avenue types. No spin doctors or advance men or headhunters. Just ordinary Moses with an extraordinary staff in his hand. And because Moses was so ordinary, so weak, when he led the Hebrews into freedom, *the whole world knew God had done it.*

We are set free within ourselves when we see our weaknesses as something in which to glory. So we boast in our affliction, for we know that God's power then rests on us.

Even if, at first, we say "no."

GOD'S GRACIOUS GIFTS TO LEADERS

JOHN C. MAXWELL

John C. Maxwell
uses the story of Moses to expound
on ten of God's enabling gifts to
His chosen leaders.

GOD'S GRACIOUS GIFTS TO LEADERS

t's hard to imagine a more impossible assignment. A nomadic sheepherder hears a strange voice coming from a burning tumbleweed, telling him to leave his sheep and goats in the wilderness, then travel to the most affluent, culturally sophisticated country in the world for the purpose of negotiating the liberation of an entire race of people held in slavery. He has no army, no air force, not even an automatic weapon or a hand grenade with which to make his point.

If that weren't enough of a challenge, this sheepherder was also a fugitive from that country, having fled many years earlier to escape standing trial for murder.

Even the makers of today's action thriller movies would find such a plot too far-fetched for production. But this implausible event is not the product of some screenwriter's overcaffeinated imagination; it's a historical reality.

Moses, the Hebrew slave turned Egyptian prince turned shepherd fugitive, executed perhaps the greatest example of leadership in world history. He did not volunteer for the job. He had not climbed any ladder or planned his career path in order to get to the position.

By examining the life of Moses in the Scriptures, and after seeing those Scriptures come to life in the new animated feature film *The Prince of Egypt,* I've discovered that when God chooses a leader, He gives that leader wonderful gifts. Though Moses was reluctant to lead through such impossible circumstances (as any of us would have been), he discovered firsthand how significant and sufficient these gifts are. Let me share with you ten of God's gracious gifts to leaders.

I.

WHEN GOD CHOOSES A LEADER,
HE GIVES THAT LEADER AN EMOTIONAL
INVESTMENT IN THE WORK

The story of Moses' infancy was one many of us learned in our earliest years of religious training. Moses, the son of Hebrew slaves, was placed in a tiny wicker boat by his mother, who defied Pharaoh's orders to kill all male babies. In the biblical account, his older sister, Miriam, watched him float down the Nile until he was discovered by none other than Pharaoh's daughter, who adopted the boy.

Miriam then arranged for Moses' real mother to nurse him until he was weaned, at which time he went to live in Pharaoh's household. In an ironic twist, the pharaoh who ordered the death of all Hebrew male babies was raising one of them in the royal palace!

The Bible isn't clear about how Moses discovered the reality of his lineage, but there must have come a time when he realized that the woman he called Mother was not really his own. In *The Prince of Egypt*, that revelation comes from Miriam, now grown, who shocks Prince Moses with the true story of his birth. In the scene that follows, Moses wrestles with what he has grown up believing and what he has now discovered. Ultimately he can escape the truth no longer; he is not one of the elite by birth—he is not Egyptian. He is Hebrew, one of a multitude who, for the last four hundred years, have felt the sting of the Egyptian whip.

83

Later, as Moses and his stepbrother, Rameses, are looking over plans to restore an Egyptian temple, for the first time Moses sees the brutal treatment of the slave masters; he hears the cries of agony from the Hebrew slaves. Rameses sees and hears nothing and continues poring over the construction plans. Moses is increasingly distracted by the abuse around him until he can stand it no longer. In his fury, he shoves a guard who has been terrorizing an old man. The guard falls from a platform onto the stone floor below and dies. It's at that point in the DreamWorks narrative that Moses runs away into the desert.

Years later, when God called him to be the redeemer of the Hebrew slaves, Moses possessed a deep emotional investment in the cause. The people he would seek to lead and liberate were not some unknown group; they were *his* people. Their cries for help must have been echoing in his ears for almost half a century. Moses finally came to the point that, if need be, he was willing to lay down his life for their liberation.

When I look around at the great Christian leaders of our day, I see men and women who would willingly die to advance the cause of Christ. I've met pastors of churches, both in the United States and around the world, who are making unbelievable sacrifices to lead because they are emotionally invested in their work. Their identity has become one with their calling. It cannot be otherwise if one expects to lead any worthy cause with the courage and conviction necessary to succeed against all odds. Without a heavy emotional investment, we all have our days when we would run away from our work.

2.

WHEN GOD CHOOSES A LEADER,

HE AFFIRMS THAT LEADER THROUGH OTHERS

After Moses fled from Egypt, he wandered in the Sinai Desert until finding a well in the region of Midian. There he rescued some young shepherd girls from bullies, who were trying to steal the precious water for their own flocks. The girls' father, Jethro, was impressed by Moses' bravery, and in *The Prince of Egypt* there is a moving scene where Jethro throws a banquet in Moses' honor. Moses protests, "Please, sir, I wish you wouldn't . . . I have done nothing in my life worth honoring" (POE).

Jethro reminds him of his act of bravery at the well, then

introduces a song that says, in part,

> So how do you measure the worth of a man?
>
> In wealth or strength or size?
>
> In how much he gained or how much he gave?
>
> The answer will come . . . to him who tries
>
> To look at his life through heaven's eyes. (POE)

The song is almost a prophecy of how Moses will find his life's purpose. In Exodus 4:18 (NKJV), the first person whom Moses told about his encounter with God at the burning bush was Jethro: "Moses went and returned to Jethro his father-in-law, and said to him, 'Please let me go and return to my brethren who are in Egypt, and see whether they are still alive.' And Jethro said to Moses, 'Go in peace.'"

Rather than sounding surprised or disappointed that he was losing his right-hand man, Jethro's response suggested he already knew that Moses was destined for bigger things than herding sheep in the Sinai Desert. He gave his blessing, no doubt with a rush of pleasure as he saw his son-in-law responding to the calling of God.

Jethro was not the only one to affirm God's calling of Moses. The Bible tells us that Moses' brother, Aaron, was already on his way into the desert to find him. God had somehow communicated to Aaron that a redeemer was on the way!

85

In *The Prince of Egypt,* out of spite for Moses' demand that he set the Hebrews free, Rameses orders the workload of the slaves doubled. That order has the desired effect of angering the Hebrews and making them more resentful of Moses' leadership. A slave flings a ball of mud at Moses that knocks him to his knees. He is assaulted with insults: "Why don't you go back to the desert, Moses?" "Why don't you leave us alone?" (POE). It is once again Moses' sister, Miriam, whom the Bible says was a prophetess (Ex. 15:20), who affirms Moses' calling: "God saved you from the river. He saved you in all your wanderings and even now He saves you from the wrath of Pharaoh. God will not abandon you. So don't you abandon us" (POE).

A calling from God makes an incredible impact in the life of a future leader. When I was in seventh grade, one day our Sunday school teacher, Glenn Leatherwood, said, "I'd like Phil Conrad, Junior Fowler, Steve Benner, and John Maxwell to stay after class." We were all goof-offs and figured we were in trouble for something. But he said, "I really sense that you boys are going to be used by God in a mighty way, and I'd like to pray for you this morning, asking God to keep your hearts pure, that you may grow up to be great men of God."

Years later as a senior in college, when I preached in senior chapel, I received a note from Dr. Brown, one of my professors. "It is evident to me that God's hand is on you in a significant way," he wrote. "I'll be eager to watch in the years to come and see how God uses you!"

One of God's special gifts is the affirmation of our calling that we receive from Him through others.

3.

When God Chooses a Leader, He Gives That Leader a Mentor

The relationship of Moses and Jethro is not fully developed in either *The Prince of Egypt* or the Scriptures. Yet we see enough hints to know that their relationship was much more than that of the typical son-in-law and father-in-law. When Moses arrived in Midian, he was completely unprepared for the life ahead of him. Jethro gave him a family, offering Moses his daughter Tzipporah in marriage.

It was surely Jethro who taught Moses the shepherd trade, showing him how to turn the sparse desert vegetation into wool and milk and meat. It was Jethro who taught him the skills of survival in that harsh environment—how to find water, where to seek shelter from the harsh winds. All those skills would later serve Moses well as he led his huge band of former slaves across the badlands of Sinai.

We make a mistake if we dismiss Jethro. Although he might have lacked formal education, his wisdom was evident by his very survival. He was the head of a rather large clan, a significant achievement in a climate where a crowd invited a catastrophe. Jethro must have been skilled at negotiating and bartering, building strategic alliances with other clans, and trading wool for other supplies. No doubt he passed those skills along to Moses.

We gain a key insight into the shrewd mind of Jethro much later in the biblical narrative, when he gave Moses some advice that saved Moses from a leader's most dreaded fate—"death by administration." Jethro went to visit Moses and "rejoiced for all the good which the LORD had done for Israel" (Ex. 18:9 NKJV). Jethro was so moved by the Israelites' deliverance, he acknowledged the sovereignty of Yahweh and offered a sacrifice to the true God.

But the next day, Jethro grew concerned when he saw Moses take the judgment seat and hear the people's grievances from morning till evening. His father-in-law took Moses aside and asked, in essence, "Son, why do you alone sit as judge? You'll burn out if you try to handle it alone. Delegate, man, delegate!"

Moses "heeded the voice of his father-in-law and did all that he had said" (Ex. 18:24 NKJV). As a result of Jethro's advice, Moses set up a judicial system, personally hearing only the most difficult legal cases.

Without a mentor, Moses would never have survived, much less been in a position to be mightily used by God. I encourage all young leaders to find a mentor, someone who can teach them the fundamental skills of leadership, someone who can pass along the wisdom gained over the years.

I've been so blessed by those who have been gracious enough to mentor me. Without a doubt, my father, Melvin Maxwell, has been my greatest mentor. As he served, first as a gifted pastor, then later as a district superintendent and college president, I saw godly leadership and character modeled for me every day of my life. So often in my early ministry, I'd call Dad to ask for help in dealing with an angry parishioner, to get sermon ideas, or just to hear his encouragement. A mentor truly is one of God's great gifts to leaders.

4.
WHEN GOD CHOOSES A LEADER,
HE BUILDS ON THAT LEADER'S STRENGTHS,
EXPERIENCES, AND BACKGROUND

In *The Prince of Egypt,* Moses' early spiritual examples are the court magicians. From them, he learns trickery and sleight of hand. But God redeems even that experience by later teaching him the values of character, truth, and courage.

Without his early experience as a member of Pharaoh's family, Moses would never have been able to gain an audience with Pharaoh. He'd have been viewed as some crazy shepherd with a bad case of sunstroke, and been killed immediately. And yet, without his desert training, he wouldn't have lasted a day in the Sinai wasteland. Going back even farther, had he not been born to a Hebrew slave and his wife, he would have lacked the passion necessary for such an awesome task.

I'm a third-generation preacher. One of my earliest conscious memories was knowing that God had a plan for my life. I couldn't have been more than three years old when I first sensed it, and my parents affirmed it every day of my life. Grandpa Maxwell always made a point of spending a little time alone with my brother, Larry, and me, asking about our future plans and praying over us. Everything about my heritage, my experience, and my strengths has prepared me for my role today.

5.
WHEN GOD CHOOSES A LEADER,
HE OFTEN REFINES THAT LEADER'S
CHARACTER IN OBSCURITY

I've often wondered why God chose to send Moses to the desert for *forty long years* before using him to lead the Hebrews' liberation. Although he learned the ways of the desert, that was most likely not the entire reason. God could have just as easily sent someone to Moses who could have guided him across Sinai, as happened in those old Westerns where the grizzled scout led settlers safely across the plains.

There is something unique about the leader whose early experience is honed in obscurity over many years. In that respect, leaders are like lumber. If a carpenter needs a two-by-four stud to frame a wall, a fast-growing, cheap softwood like yellow pine will do nicely. But for a fine piece of furniture like a dining room table, one that must be able to withstand decades of use and abuse, only a fine-grained hardwood like oak, maple, or hickory will do. Like that oak tree, the leader who has grown slowly but surely over the years has strength and resilience not found in those for whom success comes too easily or quickly.

Our nation has seen a number of Christian leaders self-destruct in recent years. In many cases, they have been leaders who found early success. They were in demand to speak at every conference. They might have discovered that it is often easier to lead by the winsomeness of one's personality than by the depth of one's character.

I've found that too much attention too soon can fuel unholy ambition. Too much success too soon can lead to an unbridled pride in self.

When I graduated from Bible college, I had an opportunity to serve a large, influential congregation. It was appealing in many ways. But I sensed that it was not God's will for me at that time in my life, so I declined. A few months later, I received another call, this time from a church in Hillham, Indiana. It was tiny. That first Sunday there were just three people present: an elderly woman named Maude, my wife, Margaret, and me! But I knew that was where God had called me, and for more than three years, I labored diligently in relative isolation and obscurity. Even when the church began to grow, few people wanted to hear my story. It was a lonely time. But I am so grateful that in that solitude, I became aware of some character issues that needed to be addressed, and I developed some habits of relating to God that have served me well for the past thirty years of ministry.

Over the years, I've met some incredible pastors and church leaders who have labored for most of their ministry in obscurity. They often feel insignificant because of where they serve. I'd love to help them see what God has done *in* them, even as they struggle to see what God has done *through* them.

Others have spent years doing what I call leading from the middle of the pack. They might not have had the position or gained the spotlight, yet they had a significant influence on their organizations.

92

When God calls someone to lead in obscurity, it is not a curse or a sign of His displeasure. Rather, it is an indication that He sees in us something worth refining, and He loves us enough to give us the gift of time to develop our character.

6.

WHEN GOD CHOOSES A LEADER, HE INSTILLS IN THAT LEADER THE VALUE OF HARD WORK

We speculate that Moses' early years in Pharaoh's palace were years of ease and leisure. *The Prince of Egypt* portrays Moses and Rameses leading a carefree childhood, racing chariots through the streets and pulling pranks on the high priests.

Certainly he knew nothing of the backbreaking labor of his Hebrew kin. It was only when he went to work for Jethro that he discovered what hard work really was!

I've been privileged to know some great leaders, and not surprisingly many of them learned the value of hard work early in life.

Bill Hybels, pastor of Willow Creek Community Church in South Barrington, Illinois, is one of the most high-capacity leaders I know. While just a kid, Bill worked as a laborer in his father's produce business. He tells of a time when he and his brother were responsible for unloading an entire semitrailer full of potatoes that had gone bad. They had no forklift, no pallet jack. But they managed to unload that forty-foot-long trailer, *one bag of rotten potatoes at a time.* In the process, Bill learned that even a seemingly impossible task could be overcome if he just kept at it, doing one thing at a time. Like compounding interest, the continual practice of doing the right things, methodically and systematically, yields amazing results over the years.

93

Learning to endure hardship, learning to persevere, learning to work hard and long—these are requisite skills for people who would lead. God will not sanctify laziness.

7.
WHEN GOD CHOOSES A LEADER, HE SUSTAINS THAT LEADER WITH A POWERFUL VISION

Proverbs 29:18 (KJV) advises, "Where there is no vision, the people perish." And before any group ever finds direction and hope in a vision, God must first captivate the heart of a leader with that vision.

A little more than a century ago, Dr. David Livingstone read these words by Robert Moffat concerning Africa: "From where I stand, I can see the smoke of ten thousand villages that have never heard of Christ." Like an encounter with a burning bush, those words birthed a vision in Livingstone's heart, and he spent the rest of his life on a quest to evangelize Africa. In tracing the Zambezi River to its source, Livingstone traveled eleven thousand miles on foot through uncharted jungles. To spread God's Word, he suffered unbelievable dangers and hardships. He was racked by disease, attacked by wild animals, and often menaced by hostile tribes. Repeatedly his own carriers robbed and abandoned him, yet he marched on with his Bible. He was fired to deep anger by the cruelty of the slave trade, and he became determined to crush what he called "the open sore of the world." His dedication won the hearts of the Africans and planted the seeds of emancipation in both Great Britain and the United States.

94

Henry Stanley reported that not one man in a million would have pressed on as Livingstone did, suffering so much to see his God-given vision fulfilled. On May 1, 1873, David Livingstone was found dead on his knees in the position of prayer in a dilapidated hut in an obscure village. All because he had a dream. Only a God-given vision would allow a man to accomplish what he did.

Long before the Hebrew slaves heard the sustaining vision of God's liberating plans for them, Moses heard of the promised land directly from the mouth of God: "So I have come down to deliver them out of slavery and bring them to their promised land. A land flowing with milk and honey" (POE).

With those words, Moses could see in his mind's eye the promised land, from the Mediterranean to the Transjordan plains, from Kadesh Barnea to Sidon. Moses could feel the land's cool breezes and life-giving rains. He could taste the fruit of the land. He could hear the waters of the Jordan percolating over the rocks, and the birds singing from the branches above its banks. He could smell the fires cooking the bountiful meals of a people who would know the meaning of the word *enough*.

95

He saw men and women, no longer bound by Egyptian chains, but free; no longer making bricks for Pharaoh's vanity projects, but building their own homes, tending their own crops, worshiping in their own temple.

I've often described the leader's role as that of the vision caster, the one who can accurately describe to a group their preferable future. Moses suffered many setbacks. His followers were often disgruntled and had trouble moving forward instead of backward. But Moses kept them moving toward the promised land because God had first revealed to him what it would be like. To find the means to press on, he had only to close his eyes and remember what God had shown him, then he could lead the people toward a better place.

8.

WHEN GOD CHOOSES A LEADER,
HE BRINGS OTHERS ALONGSIDE THAT LEADER
TO COMPENSATE FOR HIS WEAKNESSES

In Scripture, when God told Moses about the plans He had for him, Moses could not envision himself leading in the great endeavor because he was so self-conscious about his weaknesses. While still on Mount Horeb, he argued with God: "O my Lord, I am not eloquent, neither before nor since You have spoken to Your servant; but I am slow of speech and slow of tongue" (Ex. 4:10 NKJV).

96

Even after God promised, "I will teach you what you shall say," Moses remained unconvinced. While *The Prince of Egypt* portrays Aaron as doubtful, even fearful, the Bible tells us that Aaron was chosen by God to speak on Moses' behalf. And though *The Prince of Egypt* ends with Moses coming down from Mount Sinai, we see over and over in the biblical account how God provided hundreds of leaders to labor alongside Moses, most notably Joshua, Aaron, and Hur. Had Aaron and Hur not been there, literally holding up the arms of Moses (Ex. 17:12), Joshua and his army would have been defeated by the Amalekites.

I would never have achieved anything of significance if I had not recognized God's gift in others who could compensate for my weaknesses. For example, I derive no joy from working out the details of a project. Those closest to me, including Linda Eggers, my administrative assistant, and Dan Reiland, vice president of INJOY, are superstars when it comes to details and processes and follow-up. In fact, they let me come to the office only one day a month. They tell me that when I open the front door of an idea, it takes them the rest of the month to close the back door!

9.

When God Chooses a Leader, He Provides That Leader with All the Tools He'll Need

As Moses evaluated the immensity of the task that God was calling him to undertake, no doubt his mind was trying to ascertain the resources at his disposal: *I have no influence with Pharaoh anymore. Worse, I'm a fugitive. Well, let's see. The Hebrews . . . they don't even know me. They don't have any reason to trust my leadership. No army, no support personnel.* He might well have asked, "Lord, just exactly how am I supposed to accomplish this emancipation expedition with no tools, no help, and no influence?"

God did not give Moses what he expected. He did give him what he needed. The first resource He gave to Moses was that mysterious introduction: "Thus you shall say to the children of Israel, 'I AM has sent me to you'" (Ex. 3:14 NKJV).

Moses wasn't so sure that a cryptic name would do the trick: "Suppose they will not believe me or listen to my voice; suppose they say, 'The LORD has not appeared to you'" (Ex. 4:1 NKJV). The Lord gave Moses a second resource—his shepherd's staff now had supernatural powers. That staff became a powerful symbol of things to come for Moses.

The Prince of Egypt portrays the chilling event from Exodus 7:6–13, where Moses demonstrates God's power by dropping his staff, which turns into a snake. At Rameses' command, the Egyptian high priests Hotep and Huy begin their incantations of the names of their deities. Their song of intimidation begins,

> So you think you've got friends in high places
> With the power to put us on the run.
> Well, forgive us these smiles on our faces.
> You'll know what power is when we are done, son.
> You're playing with the big boys now. (POE)

In a frightening scene, they conjure up their own snakes, which crawl over Moses, then slither off. But even as the priests sing and strut, mocking the power of Yahweh, we see a silhouette of Moses' snake devouring the snakes of Hotep and Huy. The crowds don't notice— but Moses does. God's power has triumphed once more, even over the powers of mighty Egypt, and Moses knows he will prevail.

In addition to the revelation of God's name and the staff as a symbol of His power, God gave Moses a promise: "I will stretch out My hand and strike Egypt with all My wonders which I will do in its midst; and after that *he will let you go*" (Ex. 3:20 NKJV, emphasis added). Against the odds, God would triumph. In spite of Egypt's wealth, power, and dominance, in spite of Pharaoh's hardened heart, in spite of their oppression, the Hebrews *would* be liberated.

10.

When God Chooses a Leader, He Gives That Leader the Faith to Persevere

When God has chosen a leader and given him a vision of a better future for his people, it can be difficult to understand why that vision does not come about quickly. Who knows how many leaders have been chosen by God to make a significant difference in this world, but fell by the wayside, discouraged, disillusioned, and broken?

While I was pastor of Skyline Church in San Diego, California, God gave me a vision to relocate our growing church to a site that would accommodate our rapid expansion. God provided our mountaintop property site in a dramatic way, but for the next nine years, we hardly moved at all, hacking our way through jungles of red tape and environmental impact studies and government bureaucrats. There were times, usually late at night, when I wondered if we had misread God. But those doubts always vanished by morning, and we continued to grow where we were and see people's lives dramatically changed. The only reason I could persevere in spite of our rejection was a God-given faith that we would eventually triumph and build on our mountain.

Think of all the times Moses was rejected, threatened, and thwarted, and yet he persevered. Ten times Moses came to Pharaoh with God's demand, "Let my people go!" And each time Pharaoh refused him, reaping those horrible plagues, each of which mocked an occultic deity of Egypt.

All around Moses, his people were losing heart. No doubt they reasoned, "Surely Pharaoh, mighty Pharaoh, will never break. It will be Moses who is crushed, and after he is gone, we will be doomed to a lifetime of slave labor in Egypt!"

In the movie, just after seeing Pharaoh's magicians duplicate Moses' act of turning the Nile into blood in front of a crowd of Hebrew slaves, a dejected Aaron tells Moses, "Pharaoh still has the power over our lives" (POE).

Moses responds with quiet confidence: "Yes, Aaron. It's true. Pharaoh has the power. He can take away your food, your home, your freedom. He can take away your sons and daughters. With one word, Pharaoh can take away your very lives. But there is one thing he cannot take away from you. Your faith. Believe—for we will see God's wonders" (POE).

Without that kind of faith, God-chosen leaders falter. Without that kind of faith, God-chosen leaders give up and turn to some other life pursuit. Without that kind of faith, groups of God's people are left to wander in the darkness, with no one to lead them toward the light.

100

Moses knew his cause was just, timely, and ordained by God. That was all he needed to keep his faith strong and central in the face of constant barriers to his goals.

You know the rest of the story. After the plague of the first-born, Pharaoh gives in, allowing the slaves to go into the desert to worship. After a flurry of preparation, including the Passover meal of remembrance, the Hebrews are ready to go, leaving Goshen in a mighty parade of tribute to God. At the Red Sea, once again God uses Moses' staff to prove that He is sufficient, somehow pushing back the waters so God's chosen people can follow God's chosen leader across into Sinai.

Pharaoh, having fully realized the economic consequences of dismissing the slaves, comes after the Hebrews with his chariots, determined to drive them back to the slave camp. But in a mighty act of God's sovereignty, the waters of the Red Sea come crashing down on the Egyptian army, killing them all.

I'm struck by the contrast of leadership styles and priorities between Moses and Rameses in *The Prince of Egypt*. In an early scene, after a mischievous game of tag that results in destruction at a temple, Moses and Rameses are standing before Seti, the pharaoh. Both are in trouble, but Seti is particularly hard on Rameses, the heir to the throne.

"Do you understand the task for which your birth has destined you? The ancient traditions?" Seti asks. "When I pass into the Next

World, then you will be the morning and evening star" (POE).

Defiantly Rameses replies, "One damaged temple does not destroy centuries of tradition" (POE).

Seti fires back, "But one weak link can break the chain of a mighty destiny!"

Those words initiate a fear that haunts Rameses throughout the movie, so much so that when Moses first asks him to set the slaves free, Rameses hardens his heart and says, "I will *not* be the weak link!" (POE).

Rameses leads out of self-interest. Moses abandons self-interest in order to devote his life to God.

Rameses is driven to lead and lead harshly by the pain of a memory, by the fear of disappointing his father, by the fear of failure. His pain from the past cuts short his hope of a future.

Moses is not driven by a father's stinging criticism. He is led by the compelling vision from God to lead his people to the land of God's promises. His hope of the future redeems his painful past. What an amazing gift!

SEEING

LIFE THROUGH

HEAVEN'S EYES

DR. KENNETH BOA

Dr. Kenneth Boa
points out that we can begin today
to view life through heaven's eternal eyes,
as Moses ultimately did,
rather than through earth's temporal eyes.

SEEING LIFE THROUGH HEAVEN'S EYES

ichard's expectations were, to say the least, not high. As he sat in the doctor's office—the third doctor's office in as many weeks—he was prepared for the worst. Since he had been caught off guard so drastically by the first doctor's diagnosis, and had it confirmed by a second opinion, the reality was finally beginning to sink in. His days indeed might be numbered.

The doctor laid a stack of X rays and files on his desk, removed his reading glasses, and sat down across from Richard. The verdict was written all over his face: "Richard, after examining the X rays and tests, I have to tell you that I concur with the two opinions you've already received. The tumor's advanced state and its apparently rapid growth rate, plus its very complicated location, make it highly unlikely that anything can be done to arrest its development. I am sorry to have to tell you that, but I would be less than honest if I said anything more optimistic."

Feeling as if he were trying to run in a vat of molasses, Richard struggled to form the predictable responses that this life script called for. "Well, I guess I can't say that I'm surprised," he managed. "How much time do you think I have left?"

Thirty years of rehearsals had not made this answer any easier for the doctor. "Richard, you know this part of the equation isn't an exact science. Anything could happen. But my best advice to you would be not to count on too much beyond six months."

Six months, Richard thought as he drove home in silence, his accountant's brain kicking into gear. *A hundred and eighty days, 4,320 hours.* He caught himself before moving to minutes and seconds. *This changes everything! What am I going to do with the last six months of my life?*

A single thread in a tapestry

Though its color brightly shine

Can never see its purpose

In the pattern of the grand design.

And the stone that sits on the very top

Of the mountain's mighty face,

Does it think it's more important

Than the stones that form the base?

So how can you see what your life is worth

Or where your value lies?

You can never see through the eyes of man.

You must look at your life,

Look at your life through heaven's eyes. (POE)

These powerful words, sung in *The Prince of Egypt* by Jethro, Moses' future father-in-law, catch Moses at a time when life seems to hold little significance. He is a fugitive in the desert. Jethro's message for Moses, and for Richard, and for us, is this: life holds true significance only when viewed from the perspective of eternity. Life must be viewed "through heaven's eyes" in order to avoid the despair and futility of measuring life, or a few months of life, against the backdrop of human history.

What does it mean to see life through heaven's eyes? Take Richard (or you or me in a similar situation), for example. The way that he spends his last six months will be very revealing: the degree to which an unexpected cutting short of life changes someone's life is the degree to which his current priorities do not reflect a thoroughly biblical lifestyle. Let's face it. We already have a diagnosis of death (Heb. 9:27), and our days are numbered (Ps. 90:10). The problem is that we don't live in light of the temporal realities that could usher us into eternity today—or fifty years from now. Why does a shortened life span cause us to suddenly get serious about life's most important priorities? Is that evidence that we are failing to live with an eternal perspective each and every day? Perhaps it is.

In *The Prince of Egypt,* and probably in actuality, Moses learned that every day, every act is important. He learned to measure today from the perspective of eternity. He developed the fine art of keeping heaven in his view at all times. Scripture indicates that Moses' radar was always scanning the horizon for a glimpse of heaven (Heb.

11:26). Granted, he had his moments of vacillation early on. But when he was eighty years old, he got a "diagnosis" from God that seemed life-threatening to him. Fortunately he responded well and didn't have to make many adjustments to his perspective. For the next forty years of his life, until his death at age 120, he fine-tuned the skill of seeing life through heaven's eyes. In fact, Moses wrote a poetic prayer that revealed his perspective. In it he asked God to "teach us to number our days, that we may gain a heart of wisdom" (Ps. 90:12 NKJV).

108

Like everyone, Moses started with the gift of life—a blank slate, if you will, on which to sketch his life. But as few others in the Bible have done, and few others since then have done, Moses kept his life in focus. Perhaps what he experienced, and what he demonstrated, can narrow the gap between the temporal and the eternal in our lives. Perhaps Moses can help us see life through heaven's eyes as well.

What Moses Was Given: Life

In *The Prince of Egypt,* Yocheved's song, as she commits the baby Moses to an unknown fate on the Nile, frames one of history's most dramatic birth stories:

> Hush now, my baby.
> Be still, love, don't cry.
> Sleep as you're rocked by the stream.

Sleep and remember my last lullaby

So I'll be with you when you dream.

River, O river,

Flow gently for me

Such precious cargo you bear.

Do you know somewhere he can live free?

River, deliver him there. (POE)

Life is a gift in every case. But twice the infant Moses was saved from certain death and given a divinely orchestrated third chance at life. First, the Pharaoh commanded that all newborn baby boys among the Hebrew slaves be thrown into the Nile to die. Moses was saved from that horrible edict when his mother hid him for three months. Then she concealed him in a papyrus basket and hid him among the reeds along the edge of the Nile River. Instead of becoming crocodile fare, he attracted the attention of the members of Pharaoh's own household—and was saved a second time.

Twice his life could have ended, and twice it was spared. He was taken into the very household of the man who gave the order for all Hebrew baby boys to be killed—and he was spared a third time. The third chance at life was actually no chance at all; it was a divinely arranged rescue of a divinely appointed rescuer. The gift of life to the baby Moses would eventually result in the gift of life to hundreds of thousands of Hebrew slaves.

When did Moses learn that he was a Hebrew and not an Egyptian? When did he learn the story of his rescue by royalty? What must have been his thoughts as he contemplated the gift of life he had been given? Scripture gives us answers to none of these intriguing questions. It tells us only that Moses was a miracle baby, spared a death by drowning, and then given a life of luxury in the house of his judge and would-be executioner. Did this heritage give rise to his heavenly perspective? Who would not wonder if he had been saved for an eternal purpose given that set of circumstances at birth? Surely Moses' ability to see life through heaven's eyes was rooted in the memory of his salvation—plucked from certain destruction in the backwaters of the Nile and gradually merged into the strong current of God's redemptive plan.

While we may marvel at the drama of Moses' rescue and how it must have transformed his sense of destiny and calling, what about our own? First, the Bible says clearly that God has given believers a gift of new life (Rom. 6:23)—as if we had been born a second time (John 3:3). Second, like Moses' gift, our gift comes in the form of a rescue. Instead of being rescued from a river, we were rescued from a regime—that of the kingdom of darkness ruled over by Satan himself (Col. 1:13). And third, unlike Moses' rescue, our rescue is accompanied by an instruction manual that explains every-thing. Christians should not be confused about who saved us, why we were saved, and where we are headed. Through the indwelling

Holy Spirit and the written Word of God, we have everything necessary to keep our focus on eternal things.

Granted, there is opposition—there was for Moses and there is for us. Moses had to contend with in-depth training in one of the world's most sophisticated spiritual and intellectual environments. He had to separate the God of Abraham, Isaac, and Jacob from the gods of Egypt. And we believers today have competition for our spiritual affections as well.

MODERN WORLDVIEWS

Two modern views act like bookends on a library of worldviews:

Materialism

The view that ultimate reality is material only, held by few in Moses' day but by many in ours, says that everything in life is the result of the impersonal consequences of time and chance. There is no spiritual reality; there is only what the five senses can observe and understand. Spiritual views are tolerated, but only as crutches for people who are too weak to manage the reality of material conflict and conquest. As the Marxist-Leninist proponents declared in prerevolution Russia, "Religion is the opium of the people." That is, it dulls their senses and makes them dependent.

Modern versions of materialism are manifested by atheists (there is no God), naturalists (all of life can be explained by naturally occurring causes and effects), and humanists (the human being is the highest plane of intelligence and reason to be found).

How would a materialist approach the diagnosis of only six months to live? "When your number's up, your number's up. Let's eat, drink, and be merry since the diagnosis could be wrong. I might have only six weeks—or six days—or less!" Materialism predominates in Western cultures and affects many believers in Christ, manifested when one receives a life-altering piece of news: "I've got to get serious about my life." That's a sure sign that a person who knows life has a serious and eternal dimension has been living as if it didn't—living as a materialist, in other words.

Spiritualism

This view holds that ultimate reality is spiritual only. On the opposite end of the scale are those who believe that what we do in the physical dimension of life is only a momentary mirage since life is ultimately spiritual, though impersonal. There is nothing personally spiritual about spiritualism. Rather than a personal, spiritual God, there is an "all-that-is" (whatever that is). Any troubles in the material realm of life will gradually be absorbed into a higher plane of spirituality, as will each person.

At the next spiritualists' convention, look for these name tags: monists (reality is a unified whole; everything is one), pantheists (everything is god and god is everything), transcendentalists (spiritual intuition transcends empirical reality), and New Agers (dressed-up versions of the first three).

And how would a spiritualist handle a diagnosis of impending death? Probably with an enlightened perspective that sees it as a promotion to a higher plane of existence. The 1997 suicides of the Heaven's Gate cult members who killed themselves in order to catch a ride on a comet's tail reflect a New Age perspective on death. When life-changing disruptions occur, Christians who are infected by transcendentalism will handle them unrealistically—as if they did not matter in the grand scheme of things. They are probably already out of touch with a number of normal responsibilities in life and will probably get farther out of touch with the here and now as the there and then approaches.

Both of these false worldviews compete on opposite ends of the reality spectrum. Moses held the biblical view—the view that believers today need to hold as well.

Biblical Theism

Biblical theism is the view that ultimate reality is found in a speaking, personal Creator God. This view distinguishes the physical creation from the spiritual Being who created it. Creation is not God, and human beings are not God. God is God. God is one and God is three; unified yet diverse. God creates, judges, redeems, and restores. All truth about life and reality is found in Him. We can believe whatever He says. Both matter and spirit are important to God; both have their place. Because Moses was a biblical theist, the cries of the Hebrew slaves as heard in *The Prince of Egypt* eventually found proper understanding in his ears:

> With the sting of the whip on my shoulder
> With the salt of the sweat on my brow
> Elohim, God on High,
> Can You hear Your people cry?
> Help us now, this dark hour.
>
> Deliver us, Lord of all.
> Deliver us, hear our call.
> Remember us, here in this burning sand.
> Deliver us, there's a land
> You promised us.
> Deliver us to the promised land. (POE)

Moses agonized over the torture and slavery of his people. Their pain was a figment of no one's imagination, nor was it inconsequential. It was real, and Moses wanted to engage that reality. On the other hand, his spiritual encounter with God at a burning bush was likewise reality. And from the latter reality, he gained wisdom to attack the former. The spiritual dimension gave him impetus and direction for the material. After his burning bush encounter with

God, where he received instructions that seemed life-threatening—"Return to Pharaoh and demand the release of the Hebrew slaves"—Moses stayed on track the rest of his life. His dramatic salvation, his sense of destiny, and the spiritual lenses through which he looked at life helped him see life through heaven's eyes.

People who look at life through heaven's eyes find confirmation, not consternation, in life-threatening events—whether spiritually or physically life-threatening. They know life is a gift, and they are grateful. They know they live with a diagnosis of physical death as a result of Adam's sin, but they know Christ's resurrection from the dead ensures their own resurrection and eternal life. And they know their days are numbered, but they know a trustworthy, personal God is the One doing the counting. Moses responded to his gift of life by avoiding the spiritual snares of Egyptian worldviews. Believers today should be so faithful.

115

WHAT MOSES GAVE UP

Moses gave up a great deal to be faithful to God.

Luxury

Obstacles to keeping an eternal focus on life are not spiritual only; the lust of the flesh, the lust of the eyes, and the boastful pride of life work daily to change our view of what is valuable in life. And if you think Moses must have had it easy by living in 1500 B.C.—

before shiny cars and digital doodads were invented—well, think again. Moses lived in a lap of luxury that most of us cannot even imagine.

In *The Prince of Egypt*, after his sister, Miriam, tells Moses that he is actually a Hebrew, he retreats to the finery and security of his palace. He sings,

116

> Gleaming in the moonlight
> Cool and clean and all I've ever known
> All I ever wanted . . .
> Sweet perfumes of incense
> Graceful rooms of alabaster stone
> All I ever wanted . . .
>
> This is my home
> With my father, mother, brother
> Oh, so noble, oh so strong.
> Now I am home
> Here among my trappings and belongings
> I belong.
> If I've had my doubts and longings
> I see now I was wrong . . .
>
> I am a scion of this great house.
> A son of the proud history that's shown

Etched on every wall.

Surely this is all I ever wanted,

All I ever wanted.

All I ever wanted. (POE)

Though he lived in it, he managed to live through it as well. In
the book of Acts we have a revealing statement made by Stephen in
a speech to the Jewish Sanhedrin (the ruling council in Jerusalem):
"Pharaoh's daughter took [Moses] away and brought him up as her
own son. And Moses was learned in all the wisdom of the
Egyptians, and was mighty in words and deeds" (Acts 7:21–22
NKJV). In Moses' day, relatively speaking, it would have meant the
same as being a child of royalty would mean today. Privilege and
possessions would have been Moses' way of life. From three months
of age to the time when he turned forty, Moses was raised as a child
of the court of one of the most powerful civilizations on earth.
What would it have meant to Moses? How might it have pulled at
his heart?

Education

Although *The Prince of Egypt* doesn't emphasize this part of his life,
Stephen stated that Moses was learned in all the wisdom of the
Egyptians. Ancient writers filled their pages with traditions about the
intellectual, academic, and military prowess of Moses. Though we

can attach no factual certainty to the records, their mere existence points to ancient oral traditions about the legendary stature of the man. Both Greek and Jewish historians (for example, Philo, Strabo, and Josephus) record traditions about Moses: he was educated at Heliopolis as an Egyptian priest with the name Osarsiph; he was taught the whole range of Greek, Chaldee, and Assyrian literature; from the Egyptians he learned mathematics; he invented boats and building equipment; he was skilled in hydraulics, hieroglyphics, and surveying of land; he led a military expedition against the Ethiopians and founded a city to celebrate the victory; and on and on and on.

118

The question is not whether the Egyptians had the knowledge base represented in these traditions. Archaeology tells us they did. The question is whether Moses actually did all that the legends attribute to him, and that we do not know. But we do know on the authority of Scripture that he "was learned in all the wisdom of the Egyptians, and was mighty in words and deeds." His education probably amounted to the contemporary equivalent of advanced degrees in various fields of learning. Could Moses' education have been an obstacle to his knowing and serving God? Indeed it could have, but it wasn't.

Wealth

What did it mean materially to be in Moses' position? Probably that he would never have had to give a thought to his material provision as a child of Pharaoh's daughter. Certainly he had responsibilities, as do all members of royal families. Perhaps the best known examples today are the members of the British royal family. They are always busy, but their public duties are in no way tied to their income. Because they are royalty, their inherited wealth and birthright ensure their financial solvency in perpetuity.

Would wealth by birthright be difficult to give up? Some in history have; again, the British come to mind. Though an heir to the throne, Edward VIII abdicated his birthright in 1936 in order to obey what was for him a higher calling—marriage to a "commoner." We will soon discover that Moses, Prince of Egypt, obeyed his own higher calling and resisted the lure of Egyptian wealth. His transitional thinking is pictured dramatically in *The Prince of Egypt*. As Moses shivers in the cold desert night after fleeing Egypt as a fugitive, he realizes that his wealth was an asset only in Egypt. He strips off his princely sandals, necklace, armbands, and wig, casting them to the desert floor where the sands of seeming insignificance bury them forever.

Power

Education and wealth often led to power in the ancient world, but more often than not, power led to power. Simply being a member of a royal dynasty gave one immediate access to power. The gap between the powerful and the weak, the educated and the ignorant, and the rich and the poor was far greater in ancient days than today. Once the powerful were established, they were hard to remove. In fact, a conquering ruler from another realm was often the only way power was changed.

Moses would have had access to the potential for great power in Egypt. Could the power of a Pharaoh's family have corrupted the heart of a young prince? Without question. Moses was to discover, however, at a time when he was powerless in the world's eyes that he would become the representative of a Higher Power who would conquer Egypt. Perhaps God exposed Moses in his younger years to the great power of Egypt so that he would have an appreciation for the power of God about which he would learn so much.

A Temporal Perspective

The New Testament says that three things can fill the eyes of the Christian and keep him from seeing with an eternal view: the lust of the flesh, the lust of the eyes, and the boastful pride of life (1 John 2:16). Adam and Eve wrestled with these three in the Garden of Eden and lost (Gen. 3:1–7). Jesus Christ wrestled with the same three in the desert of Judea and won (Luke 4:1–13). Between them stood Moses who, though not perfect, "was faithful in all [God's] house" (Heb. 3:2, 5 NKJV). How did Moses do it? The writer to the Hebrews told us: "Moses, when he became of age, refused to be called the son of Pharaoh's daughter [pictured as Pharaoh's wife in

The Prince of Egypt], choosing rather to suffer affliction with the people of God than to enjoy the passing pleasures of sin, esteeming the reproach of Christ greater riches than the treasures in Egypt; for he looked [ahead] to the reward" (Heb. 11:24–26 NKJV).

Moses discovered the secret to living a consistent spiritual life. Perhaps looking ahead is the key. Anyone who has had the experience of tripping over a small stone while gazing at a granite mountain can understand Moses' secret. Education, wealth, power— Moses was raised, and lived, in the lap of luxury. But the privileges were only minor obstacles to One who knew his destination. Somehow—and we don't really know how—God had communicated to Moses enough to keep him from drowning in the ocean of Egyptian culture. Saved first from the world's longest river, and saved last from the world's most powerful culture, Moses looked ahead to his reward.

For the Christian today to follow Moses' example, a paradigm shift must occur. A paradigm is a way of seeing based on implicit or explicit rules that shape one's perspective. A paradigm shift takes place when the rules or boundaries change so that we no longer see things from the same perspective. When the rules change, our way of seeing is altered. The proof from Copernicus (1473–1543) that the world revolved around the sun, and not the opposite, was perhaps the grandest example of a paradigm shift. Talk about the need to take a deep breath! But the need of Middle Agers to reassess their

121

worldview was not much greater than the need of some modern middle-agers to do the same. Many of us view life through the wrong paradigm—an earthly rather than a heavenly one.

Suppose someone plans to move from Dallas to Atlanta where he knows he will spend the remaining fifty years of his life. He laboriously plans and itemizes every detail of the two-day trip without giving any thought to his ultimate destination. The absurdity of this scenario is easy to see, and yet most of the people we encounter are really living their lives in this way. In this analogy, the two-day trip is our earthly sojourn, and the fifty-year stay is our eternal destiny. But what is obviously ludicrous on a temporal scale somehow seems acceptable when we speak of eternity, perhaps because our eternal destiny seems so vague and wispy.

We can expect to encounter this ongoing struggle for the remainder of our worldly sojourn. May it be said of us that, like Moses, we look ahead.

What Moses Got: Liabilities

One of the greatest misconceptions among contemporary Christians is that the spiritual experience is akin to a cosmic swap fest or flea market. We bring our goods (faith and followership) and God brings His (promises and power), and the bartering begins. We offer God our faith and allegiance in return for a life free of inconvenience, requirement, and sacrifice. The problem with this scenario is that it takes two parties to barter, and God has no intention of being one of them.

An entire chapter in the Bible is devoted to the principle that faith can be a very difficult thing. A cursory read of Hebrews 11 by a young Christian will be an immediate warning: if all the famous Bible characters that I heard about in Sunday school went through great difficulties in their faith, what does it say about me? It says that a relationship with God can lead from luxury to liability—just as it did with Moses.

Did Jesus Christ leave the glory of heaven and end up on a cross? Did Abraham leave cosmopolitan Babylon and end up in rural Palestine and later in jail? Did David go from being anointed king of Israel to being pursued and hunted like a wild dog? Did Paul the apostle leave the pride and prestige of Judaism and find himself shipwrecked in the Mediterranean? Yes to all of the above. And Moses was about to make his own journey from luxury to liability. But like the others in the Hebrews 11 Hall of Faith, he never took his eyes off the goal.

As already noted, we have fewer details about Moses' developmental years in Egypt than we would like. We are told in Scripture, however, that Moses killed an Egyptian official or soldier who was beating a Hebrew, "one of his brethren" (Ex. 2:11 NKJV). So at that time in his life Moses knew that he was a Hebrew, and his heart was toward his own people. Out of compassion for a Hebrew slave, he mortally wounded an Egyptian attacker. But the act of solidarity not only earned the resentment of his brethren, who thought he was trying to become their leader (Ex. 2:14); it also earned the wrath of the pharaoh, who attempted to kill him (Ex. 2:15). Moses fled Egypt and found himself in the dry and barren land of Midian, east of Egypt near the Red Sea.

124

For forty years (Acts 7:29–30), Moses exchanged the desserts of Egypt for the deserts of Midian. An outcast and a fugitive, Moses had a long time to ponder the purposes of the God of the Hebrews. Was that why he was saved from death as an infant? Was that why he was trained in all the wisdom of the Egyptians? Was that why he carried a sense of destiny and Hebrew heritage in his heart? To live in the outback of Midian as a shepherd?

If those liabilities were not enough, after the pharaoh who pursued Moses died, God commissioned Moses to return to Egypt and lead the Hebrew slaves to the land promised to Abraham. That was Moses' reward for years of faithfulness to God? And yet, because his eye was still on the prize, Moses returned to Egypt.

The next forty years of Moses' life turned out to be unbelievably difficult, if not actually comical at times. Instead of having a handful of liabilities, Moses became the leader of a couple of million of them. His assignment: lead a weak, bedraggled, inexperienced, ill-prepared, and discontented group of slaves across a parched desert, forming them into a unified nation complete with religious practices, a moral and civil law code, and a spirit of cooperation and unity. Oh, and don't forget to feed them along the way and provide food and water for their livestock. And Moses was faithful as a servant (Heb. 3:5). In fact, God was so confident in dealing with Moses that He spoke face-to-face with him, not in visions and in dreams as He did with others (Num. 12:6–8).

It has often been said that the greater the responsibility God gives, the more intense and clear His communications will be. Perhaps that was the reason for God's face-to-face exchanges with Moses, to keep him focused on the path to the promised land. At least ten times in the first twenty-four months following the Exodus, the Israelites expressed their displeasure (read "rebellion") toward God and His plan for their lives (Num. 14:22). And who, besides God, caught the brunt of their rebellious ways? Moses, the former prince in the court of Pharaoh, who had probably never had anyone disobey or grumble at him in his life.

Though Moses' story as told in *The Prince of Egypt* does not picture the forty years of his life after the Exodus, those years were the most trying of all. Surely Moses was tempted to wonder whether seeing life through heaven's eyes was always possible, especially since the people he was leading seemed to have eyes for nothing except food, water, and their personal comfort.

- Barely out of Egypt, the Hebrews rebelled at the Red Sea when they saw Pharaoh's army approaching (Ex. 14:10–12).

- The people grumbled about not having fresh water to drink (Ex. 15:22–24).

- The promise of milk and honey wasn't enough to keep them from grumbling about missing their Egyptian gruel (Ex. 16:1–3).

- Not willing to trust God's daily provision of manna, the people disobeyed and hoarded the manna (Ex. 16:19–20).

- Afraid God wouldn't provide on the first day of the week, the people disobeyed Moses' instructions about the Sabbath (Ex. 16:27–30).

- There was more complaining about water rights—their right to have some (Ex. 17:1–4).

- Serious rebellion began. The people, along with Aaron, who knew better, created a golden calf to worship when they thought Moses abandoned them (Ex. 32:1–35).

- After a year of experiencing God's provision and presence at Sinai, the people hit the road complaining again—and God sent judgment (Num. 11:1–3).

- After that incident, some rabble among the people began rabble-rousing, causing complaints about the food—again (Num. 11:4–34).

- The last straw came at Kadesh, when Moses sent twelve

men into Canaan to explore the land. Ten of the twelve
came back petrified with fear and threw the people into
panic and confusion. Even on the doorstep of their new
home, they wanted to go back to Egypt. At least part of
their desire was granted. Rather than being forced into a
land for which they had no faith, everyone over age twenty
was sentenced to die in the wilderness within sight of God's
promised land (Num. 14).

127

As if two or three million faithless former slaves weren't enough
to be on guard against, Moses had one even larger liability than all
of their natures put together. He had to be on guard against his own
sinful nature. Moses learned the hard way that no one's sins are as
looming a liability as one's own. As faithful as Moses was as a servant in God's house, even he failed to obey God on one occasion
(Num. 20:1–13). And because Moses' responsibilities brought
intense communication from God, his disobedience brought intense
judgment. Moses would not enter the promised land.

If Moses had known about the impending liabilities associated with
God's call on his life, would he still have responded? I believe he would
have. There is sufficient evidence in Scripture to indicate that Moses
could tell the difference between temporal roadblocks and eternal
rewards. No amount of Sinai sand could block Moses' vision in the
wilderness. Even there, he succeeded at viewing life through heaven's eyes.

What Moses Gained: Life Eternal

Besides the trying period of adolescence, most people experience another watershed time around midlife. Somewhere between ages forty and fifty it becomes necessary to face up to life and make adjustments and plans that will ensure a significant second half of life. Call it a midlife crisis or any other label—it amounts to the weighing of two value systems. By midlife, most people have experimented with facets of "the good life" and know what it stands for. The Christian at midlife should be able to see clearly the difference between a temporal value system and an eternal value system. The Christian who gradually chooses the latter as his lifestyle is the believer who follows the example of Moses.

128

Why was Moses able to persevere in the wilderness? And why was the loss of his personal goal of reaching the promised land not a life-shattering tragedy for him? Because, as we have seen, he had his eye on a different prize: "He looked [ahead] to the reward . . . He endured as seeing Him who is invisible" (Heb. 11:26–27 NKJV).

In *The Prince of Egypt*, Moses' sister, Miriam, encourages him to focus his eyes by faith, not by sight, as the task of leading the Hebrew slaves out of Egypt looms before him. She sings,

Many nights we've prayed

With no proof anyone could hear.

In our hearts a hopeful song

We barely understood.

Now we are not afraid

Although we know there's much to fear.

We were moving mountains

Long before we knew we could.

There can be miracles

When you believe.

Though hope is frail

It's hard to kill.

Who knows what miracles

You can achieve

When you believe?

Somehow you will,

You will when you believe. (POE)

129

It seems that heavenly rewards are part of the formula for looking at life through heaven's eyes. Jesus Christ mentioned that in
Matthew 6:1–18 a number of times. In the passage, He basically
said that rewards are available in two places: earth and heaven. You
can live your life in such a way on this earth so as to receive the
acclaim and honor of men, and you will have your reward as a result.
Or you can live your life in such a way that pleases God and receive
your reward from Him in heaven. The question then is this: Why

would any believer in Christ pursue a value system that led to a few years of rewards from other human beings when rewards from God can be enjoyed forever?

Moses seemed to have discerned this difference and made his decision accordingly. The prize that his eye was on was not the acclaim of men, but the approval of God. Why could he listen to the constant grumblings of the Hebrew people in the wilderness? Because God had asked him to. Why could he submit obediently to God's decision to end his life before a significant personal goal was met? Because it was God's decision. And Moses knew that no earthly achievement or pleasure—whether protecting himself from willful wilderness wanderers or entering the promised land—could possibly carry the same eternal value as pleasing God. Just as two rival worldviews compete for man's affections, so two rival value systems do as well: the temporal value system and the eternal value system. Moses chose the latter; which one do you choose?

Each of us is required to make a choice. Which will we believe? How consistent is our behavior with our belief? If we receive a diagnosis of six months to live and our lives change radically, two value systems are most likely at war within us. The crucial contrast lies in where these opposing value systems ultimately lead:

TEMPORAL VALUE SYSTEM	ETERNAL VALUE SYSTEM
(Seeing Life Through Earth's Eyes)	*(Seeing Life Through Heaven's Eyes)*
Pleasure	Knowing God
Recognition of people	Approval of God
Popularity	Servanthood
Wealth and status	Integrity and character
Power	Humility

Consider all the things Moses didn't receive during his 120 years on earth, especially during the last 80 years of his adulthood: fame, fortune, the appreciation of the people he served, the admiration of leaders of other nations, a comfortable retirement home in the promised land. But think of what he did receive: the approval of his God. Moses, like Abel, Enoch, Noah, Abraham, Isaac, Jacob, and Joseph before him (Heb. 11:1–22), missed out on much in this life in order to gain much in the next.

A paraphrase of Hebrews 11:13–16 is a perfect description of the eternal value system of the man Moses:

> Moses was living by faith when he died. He did not receive the things promised; he only saw them and welcomed them from a distance. He admitted that he was an alien and a stranger on earth. People who say such things show that they are looking for a country of their own. If Moses had

been thinking of the country he had left, he would have had opportunity to return. Instead, he was longing for a better country—a heavenly one. Therefore God is not ashamed to be called Moses' God, for He has prepared a city for him.

132

Could your name be substituted in those verses for the name of Moses? Could mine? Would God be ashamed to be called our God?

The next time the pressure of competing worldviews and value systems begins to tempt you to see life through earth's eyes instead of heaven's eyes, let God do for you what He did for Moses. When it was time for his earthly life to end, Moses climbed Mount Nebo, on the east side of the Jordan River. There, God showed him the promised land, the land that the Israelites would inherit, the land that he would not touch with his foot. And it was acceptable to Moses and to the Lord. As friends, they agreed together that missing some earthly gain can in no way compare with gaining all of heaven.

Through which eyes are you viewing life? Since that day on Mount Nebo, "there has not arisen in Israel a prophet like Moses" (Deut. 34:10 NKJV). We may not be prophets like Moses, but we can begin today to view life through his—and heaven's—eyes.

So how can you see what your life is worth
Or where your value lies?

You can never see through the eyes of man.

You must look at your life,

Look at your life through heaven's eyes. (POE)

THE
VOICE FROM THE
MOP BUCKET

MAX LUCADO

*Our habit of settling for broken
dreams can be changed in a surprising instant,
as Moses' was by a voice from a burning bush.
You never know, Max Lucado says,
because "God ain't finished with you yet."*

The Voice from the Mop Bucket

he hallway is silent except for the wheels of the mop bucket and the shuffle of the old man's feet. Both sound tired.

Both know these floors. How many nights has Hank cleaned them? Always careful to get in the corners. Always careful to set up his yellow caution sign warning of wet floors. Always chuckling as he does. "Be careful, everyone," he says and laughs to himself, knowing no one is near.

Not at 3:00 A.M.

Hank's health isn't what it used to be. Gout keeps him awake. Arthritis makes him limp. His glasses are so thick, his eyeballs look twice their size. His shoulders stoop. But he does his work. Slopping soapy water on linoleum. Scrubbing the heel marks left by the well-heeled lawyers. He'll be finished an hour before quitting time. Always finishes early. Has for twenty years.

When he has finished, he'll put away his bucket and take a seat outside the office of the senior partner and wait. Never leaves early. Could. No one would know. But he doesn't.

He broke the rules once. Never again.

Sometimes, if the door is open, he'll enter the office. Not for long. Just to look. The suite is larger than his apartment. He'll run his finger over the desk. He'll stroke the soft leather couch. He'll stand at the window and watch the gray sky turn gold. And he'll remember.

138

He once had such an office.

Back when Hank was Henry. Back when the custodian was an executive. Long ago. Before the night shift. Before the mop bucket. Before the maintenance uniform. Before the scandal.

Hank doesn't think about it much now. No reason to. Got in trouble, got fired, and got out. That's it. Not many people know about it. Better that way. No need to tell them.

It's his secret.

Hank's story, by the way, is true. I changed the name and a detail or two. I gave him a different job and put him in a different century. But the story is factual. You've heard it. You know it. When I give you his real name, you'll remember.

But more than a true story, it's a common story. It's a story of a derailed dream. It's a story of high hopes colliding with harsh realities.

Happens to all dreamers. And since all have dreamed, it happens to us all.

In Hank's case, it was a mistake he could never forget. A grave mistake. Hank killed someone. He came upon a thug beating up an innocent man, and Hank lost control. He killed the mugger. When word got out, Hank got out.

Hank would rather hide than go to jail. So he ran. The executive became a fugitive.

True story. Common story. Most stories aren't as extreme as Hank's. Few spend their lives running from the law. Many, however, live with regrets.

139

"I could have gone to college on a golf scholarship," a fellow told me just last week on the fourth tee box. "Had an offer right out of school. But I joined a rock-and-roll band. Ended up never going. Now I'm stuck fixing garage doors."

"Now I'm stuck." Epitaph of a derailed dream.

Pick up a high school yearbook and read the "What I want to do" sentence under each picture. You'll get dizzy breathing the thin air of mountaintop visions:

"Ivy League school."
"Write books and live in Switzerland."
"Physician in a Third World country."
"Teach inner-city kids."

Yet take the yearbook to a twentieth-year reunion and read the next chapter. Some dreams have come true, but many haven't. Not that all should, mind you. I hope the little guy who dreamed of being a sumo wrestler came to his senses. And I hope he didn't lose his passion in the process. Changing direction in life is not tragic. Losing passion in life is.

Something happens to us along the way. Convictions to change the world downgrade to commitments to pay the bills. Rather than make a difference, we make a salary. Rather than look forward, we look back. Rather than look outward, we look inward.

140

And we don't like what we see.

Hank didn't. Hank saw a man who'd settled for the mediocre. Trained in the finest institutions of the world, yet working the night shift in a minimum-wage job so he wouldn't be seen in the day.

But all that changed when he heard the Voice from the mop bucket. (Did I mention that his story is true?)

THE VOICE

At first he thought the Voice was a joke. Some of the fellows on the third floor play these kinds of tricks.

"Henry, Henry," the Voice called.

Hank turned. No one called him Henry anymore.

"Henry, Henry."

He turned toward the pail. It was glowing. Bright red. Hot red. He could feel the heat ten feet away. He stepped closer and looked in. The water wasn't boiling.

"This is strange," Hank mumbled to himself as he took another step to get a closer look. But the Voice stopped him.

"Don't come any closer. Take off your shoes. You are on holy tile."

Suddenly Hank knew who was speaking. "God?"

I'm not making this up. I know you think I am. Sounds crazy. Almost irreverent. God speaking from a hot mop bucket to a janitor named Hank? Would it be believable if I said God was speaking from a burning bush to a shepherd named Moses?

141

Maybe that one's easier to handle because you've heard it before. But just because it's Moses and a bush rather than Hank and a bucket, it's no less spectacular.

It sure shocked the sandals off Moses. We wonder what amazed the old fellow more: that God spoke in a bush or that God spoke at all.

Moses, like Hank, had made a mistake.

You remember his story, depicted so stirringly in *The Prince of Egypt*. Adopted nobility. An Israelite reared in an Egyptian palace, brother to the pharaoh's son, Rameses. His countrymen were slaves, but Moses was privileged. Ate at the royal table. Educated in the finest schools.

In the film, the court magicians teach Moses. But Scripture tells us that his most influential teacher was his mother, Yocheved. A Jewess who was hired to be his nanny. "Moses," you can almost hear her whisper to her young son, "God has put you here on purpose. Someday you will set your people free. Never forget, Moses. Never forget." In the film, Moses' sister, Miriam, echoes this theme, singing, "Grow, baby brother. Come back someday, come and . . . deliver us . . . too" (POE). When she and Moses meet as adults, she awakens all those memories, insisting, "God saved you to be our deliverer" (POE).

And Moses remembers. The flame of justice grows hotter until it blazes. Moses sees an Egyptian beating a Hebrew slave. Just like Hank kills the mugger, Moses kills the Egyptian.

In Scripture, the next day Moses saw the Hebrew (Ex. 2:14). You'd think the slave would say thanks. He didn't. Rather than express gratitude, he expressed anger. "Will you kill me too?" he asked.

GOD AIN'T FINISHED WITH YOU YET

Moses knew he was in trouble. He turned his back on all he'd ever wanted, all he'd ever known, as he sings in *The Prince of Egypt*, and fled Egypt and hid in the wilderness. Call it a career shift. He went from dining with the heads of state to counting heads of sheep.

Hardly an upward move.

And so it happened that a bright, promising Hebrew—the Prince of Egypt—began herding sheep in the hills. From the Ivy League to the cotton patch. From the Oval Office to a taxicab. From swinging a golf club to digging a ditch.

Moses thought the move was permanent. There is no indication he ever intended to go back to Egypt. In fact, there is every indication he wanted to stay with his sheep. As *The Prince of Egypt* depicts

142

it, standing barefoot before the bush, he asks, "Who am I to lead these people?" (POE).

I'm glad Moses asked that question. It's a good one. Why Moses? Or more specifically why the older Moses?

The younger version was more appealing. The Moses we saw in Egypt was brash and confident. In the film, he races wildly in his chariot through the streets of Egypt and drops water balloons on the court magicians. But the Moses we found years later in the desert was reluctant and weather-beaten.

143

Had you or I looked at Moses back in Egypt, we would have said, "This man is ready for battle." Educated in the finest system in the world, according to Scripture. Trained by the ablest soldiers. Instant access to the inner circle of the pharaoh. Moses spoke their language and knew their habits. He was the perfect man for the job.

Younger Moses we liked. But older Moses? No way. Too tired. Smelled like a shepherd. Spoke like a foreigner. What impact would he have on Pharaoh? He was the wrong man for the job.

And Moses would have agreed. "Tried that once before," he would say. "Those people don't want to be helped. Just leave me here to tend my sheep. They're easier to lead."

Moses wouldn't have gone. You wouldn't have sent him. I wouldn't have sent him.

But God did. How do you figure? Benched as a younger man and suited up as an older man. Why? What did Moses know that he didn't know before? What had he learned in the desert that he didn't learn in Egypt?

The ways of the desert, for one. Young Moses was a city boy. Older Moses knew the name of every snake and the location of every watering hole. If he was going to lead thousands of Hebrews into the wilderness, he better know the basics of Desert Life 101.

Family dynamics, for another. If he was going to be traveling with families for forty years, it might help to understand how they work. He married Tzipporah, a woman of faith, the daughter of a Midianite priest, and established his own family.

But more than the ways of the desert and the people, Moses needed to learn something about himself.

Apparently he had learned it. God said Moses was ready.

And to convince him, God spoke through a bush. (Had to do something dramatic to get Moses' attention.) "I have come down to deliver them out of slavery," God says in *The Prince of Egypt*, "and bring them to their promised land . . . And so unto Pharaoh I shall send you" (POE).

In other words, "School's out. Now it's time to get to work." Poor Moses. He didn't even know he was enrolled.

But he was. And guess what? So are you. The Voice from the bush is the voice that whispers to you. It reminds you that God is not finished with you yet. It assures you, as God's voice does in the film, "I shall be with you" (POE). Oh, you may think God is finished with you. You may think you've peaked. You may think He's got someone else to do the job.

If so, think again.

"God began doing a good work in you, and I am sure he will continue it until it is finished when Jesus Christ comes again" (Phil. 1:6 NCV).

Did you see what God is doing? *A good work in you.*

Did you see when He will be finished? *When Jesus comes again.*

May I spell out the message? *God ain't finished with you yet.*

Your Father wants you to know that. And to convince you, He may surprise you. He may speak through a bush or a mop bucket, or stranger still, He may speak through this book.

145

THE ENABLING POWER OF GOD IN THE LIVES OF HIS CHILDREN

THELMA WELLS

*God uses ordinary people
(like Moses) and ordinary things
(like Moses' staff) to accomplish His purposes.
Thelma Wells reiterates this truth
as she parallels many of her life's challenges
to those of Moses.*

THE ENABLING POWER
OF GOD IN THE LIVES
OF HIS CHILDREN

od can take a "nobody"—a person society discounts as not having the ability, skills, or opportunity to amount to anything—and make him a "somebody." God can use a person with flaws, fears, and weaknesses to accomplish great missions in life. He can empower a demure, insecure, frail person with assurance and strength to set a whole nation free from bondage. I know. He did it for Moses.

When I consider Moses' attributes, I think of his fears and his accomplishments. Although Moses became one of God's greatest leaders, he first had to overcome his fears. He was afraid to accept God's calling as a leader, afraid to witness to the Israelites for fear that they would not believe him. He was even afraid to speak out in public. When God called Moses to lead His people out of Israel, Moses made excuse after excuse. By our standards, Moses answered somewhat like a wimp. But God's vision and mission for him were greater than his fears. God made his weaknesses become his strengths.

Moses and I have a lot in common:

- We are both from slavery ancestry. Moses was an Israelite whose people were oppressed by the Egyptians for some four hundred years. I am an African-American whose people were enslaved in America for two hundred years.

- We were both raised by surrogate mothers. Moses was raised as the prince of Egypt by Pharaoh's daughter (Pharaoh's wife in the film *The Prince of Egypt*), who knew Moses was a Hebrew, but who loved and cared for him as her own son despite his heritage. I was raised by my great-grandmother and great-grandfather, Sarah and William Harrell, who rescued me from poverty when my mother, unwed and seventeen years old, could not care for me. I was loved and tenderly cared for despite my illegitimacy.

- We were both rescued from life-threatening situations. Pharaoh had given orders to all his people: "Every son who is born you shall cast into the river, and every daughter you shall save alive" (Ex. 1:22 NKJV). Fearing for her baby boy's life, Moses' mother hid him for three months until the day Pharaoh's daughter found him in the bulrushes near the palace and took him in as her adopted son. As seen in the film *The Prince of Egypt*, Moses' adopted mother cherishes him. He grows up in a happy environment—playing with his brother, Rameses, and respecting his father, Seti. Moses believes that they are his birth family, and he loves them very much. When I was two years old, I went to live with my great-grandparents because both my mother and I were very ill at the time. Grannie asked if she could keep me until I was well. She took me to live with her and Daddy Harrell in their garage apartment, and even after I recovered, I never went back to my mother. I did go to visit her often during my childhood, but after each visit, I was always more than ready to return to the garage apartment. Nothing could have persuaded me that their warm and cozy apartment on Thomas Avenue was not my rightful home.

- Both our lives changed after forty. When Moses was about forty years old, he saw an Egyptian beating an Israelite; he flew into a rage and killed the Egyptian. Afraid that Pharaoh would execute him, Moses fled into the Midian Desert. He got married, had children, and lived the lifestyle of a shepherd. He said, "I have been a stranger in a foreign land" (Ex. 2:22 NKJV). After Moses had lived in Midian for about forty years, the Lord appeared to him in a burning bush to give him his mission in life: to lead his people out of Egypt and slavery and lead them into the promised land. When I was forty years old, my whole life changed too. I had been a bank officer for several years. I was satisfied with the status I had achieved in my position as assistant vice president for customer service. But God put a yearning in my spirit that I could not shake. It was 1984. I left a guaranteed salary, a pension plan, medical benefits, and paid vacation to pursue public speaking and teaching full-time. At first, my classes were all bank related. But as I grew in Jesus, my message began to take form in a simple motto that I have used ever since, "In Christ, you can be the best of what you want to BEE!"

Now please don't think I'm bragging. I make these comparisons with Moses not to boast, but to illustrate God's enabling power in the lives of His children. If it was not for God, Moses would not have led his people out of bondage, and I certainly would not have had the courage to witness to people from all walks of life about God's grace.

God's power is awesome. It has enabled me to depend on Him even when I feared His mission for me. I've had times in my profession when I just didn't know what to say or how to say it. I've been overcome with frustration waiting on God to answer, and I've even felt discouraged. But through it all, I've learned to depend upon Him, and He has never failed me. He didn't fail Moses. And He will not fail you either.

GOD'S ENABLING POWER
WHEN YOU FEAR HIS CALLING

You've chosen the wrong messenger.
How can I even speak to these people?
—Moses, speaking to God (POE)

153

Some people accept God's calling without question. I've met preachers who said they couldn't wait to start their ministry. I've met missionaries who gladly entered the mission field at God's beckoning. Others have told me that they are anxiously anticipating God's calling, and whatever He wants of them, they are willing and ready to serve. Not me!

When God called me to minister, I was enjoying the comfort of teaching my Sunday school class and attending Bible study. I liked singing in the choir and going to prayer meetings. St. John Missionary Baptist is a beautiful, respected church in the Dallas community, and many of my lifelong friends grew up with me right there. I took pleasure in spending time with my well-dressed, well-educated, and well-rounded friends and church members. In other words, I was satisfied in the comfort and grandeur of my little world of Christianity. I was complacent in my little world of church.

I'm not proud of this, but I remember telling my Sunday school class, "I just can't totally submit to God. I'm too scared. He may ask me to go to Africa, and I don't like flies. If I totally submit to God, I don't know where He'll send me. I don't want to leave home. I don't want to lead the lifestyle of a missionary. I'm just not ready to turn everything over to God!"

I was really scared to relinquish my total self to God's calling on my life. I believed that if I did, He would give me a task that I just didn't want. I was selfish. I figured God didn't know me as well as I knew myself. I was wrong.

God called Moses after he had spent forty long, hard years in the land of Midian. Moses had been prepared during that time to accomplish the tasks ahead of him. He had learned patience, temperance, and humility. God had used the years to shape his mind and his ways. It's funny how God prepares us for our mission and many times we don't even have a clue.

I had been blessed with a contract teaching position for the American Institute of Banking. For more than ten years, I taught banking students customer service skills. During that time, I started my speaking business where I spoke to all kinds of organizations including banks, colleges and universities, corporations, civic and community groups, churches, and other religious organizations. I spoke on a variety of human relations topics, such as customer service, cultural diversity, dealing with difficult people. From the speaking engagements, I had the opportunity to begin writing books. I traveled throughout North America and many foreign countries, leading a life that should have been completely satisfying, a life that would seem to bring total self-actualization. But it didn't. Something was missing.

In 1990, I realized that I sorely needed something else in my life. I was not being fulfilled. I had been a Christian since the age of four, so it wasn't salvation. I prayed and studied my Bible; I attended church regularly. I enjoyed speaking. But the nagging emptiness in my spirit needed to be filled. Often I prayed, "Lord, show me what You want me to do!"

Early in the spring of 1995 on a Saturday night I was sitting on my bed having a conversation with the Lord. I was moved to lie flat on the floor and just listen to what God had to say. I was always talking to Him, but I knew that night that He wanted my attention so that He could talk directly to me. God spoke clearly (not audibly), but in my mind and soul He said: *My child, your life is about to change drastically. The changes are for the better. I have heard your longing to do more for Me. Everything will not run smoothly. You will have some health issues, but do not worry, they are only temporary. Your lifestyle will change. You will come in contact with people you've never heard of before.*

I don't know how long He talked to me, but I do know that I wanted to make sure it was the Lord and not me talking to myself. So I asked Him to prove to me that He was speaking. In my mind and soul He spoke these words: *Get up and wash your face and get in the bed. Your husband will be home in exactly five minutes.*

I got up, washed my face, and waited for George. In exactly five minutes, he drove into the driveway. I had been crying, partially because I was overwhelmed with joy that God would talk with me in such a way, and partially because I was a little frightened. I still had questions about what was going to happen.

I had been afraid to totally submit to God, but somehow on the floor that evening, it seemed easier. I knew that the Holy Spirit could and would work through me to carry out a mission that would glorify God. There was no need to fear His calling anymore. All my anxious fears about the future were gone. God was now in charge of my life.

Many of us are like Moses when God calls our names. We make excuses, deny our readiness, and protest God's confidence in us. But God wants us to know that He is present and active in our lives. Moses did go back to Egypt to convey God's message: "Let my people go" (POE). I waited a few more years for a clearer vision of my mission. But the difference was, I was willing to go.

GOD'S ENABLING POWER
WHEN YOU NEED A MESSAGE
Me? Who am I to lead these people?
They'll never believe me. They won't even listen!
—Moses, speaking to God (POE)

Have you ever wondered if you are saying the right thing? Have you ever felt that you just might be sticking your foot in your mouth? Well, once God revealed to me that He had a purpose and a mission for me to fulfill, I knew I needed a message. There is nothing worse than speaking to people and knowing that they are not listening. I thought, *How can I give them a word that they will remember?*

One Sunday I was walking down the church steps when my friend, Mary Jo Evans, stopped me to admire the gold bee pinned to the lapel of my suit.

"Thelma Wells, that sure is a pretty bee," she said. "Every time you wear that, remember that you can 'bee' the best at whatever you want to 'be-e-e.' " She stretched out the one-syllable word, smiling as she spoke. I couldn't mistake her meaning.

That's it, I thought. *That's the symbol I've been looking for, and it's been pinned on my shoulder all the time.* I'd been conducting seminars and lecturing for several years at that point. But I was praying for a logo I could use to represent my theme. I needed a handle people could grab hold of—something they could take with them as a constant reminder when they left my seminars. That day, Mary Jo gave me the idea to use the bumblebee as my symbol. I knew deep down within this was the message of hope that God wanted me to carry to everybody I came in contact with.

The fact that scientists and aeronautical engineers can't explain the unlikely flight of the bumblebee makes it an even more appropriate symbol for me. This black, illegitimate child of a disabled teenager, born more than two decades before the passage of the Civil Rights Bill—why would anyone listen to me? Would anyone really expect me to get my messages off the ground?

158

When God spoke to Moses from the flames of a burning bush, He gave him several messages. To Pharaoh, he was to say, "Let my people go." Then to the Israelites, Moses was to say, "The LORD God of your fathers, the God of Abraham, the God of Isaac, and the God of Jacob, has sent me to you" (Ex. 3:15 NKJV). But Moses thought, *Why would anyone listen to me?* He complained, "O my Lord, I am not eloquent, neither before nor since You have spoken to Your servant; but I am slow of speech and slow of tongue" (Ex. 4:10 NKJV).

But God's answer to Moses was loud and clear: "Who has made man's mouth? Or who makes the mute, the deaf, the seeing, or the blind? Have not I, the LORD? Now therefore, go, and I will be with your mouth and teach you what you shall say" (Ex. 4:11–12).

Many times in my career I have needed to be reminded that God will teach me what to say, though some may not like what they hear.

I was asked to speak at some of the Women of Faith conferences. I had been invited by a staff member who had read my book *Bumblebees Fly Anyway: Defying the Odds at Work and Home.* She said that she was fascinated by my book and was convinced that I was the person God had appointed to become one of the speakers for the conference. In prayer, I accepted the invitation to speak in August, September, and October 1996.

Preparing to speak at the first conference was not easy. Although I had delivered my bumblebee metaphor many times, I prayed and asked God to give me a fresh message for the women at that particular conference. The message I received frightened me. It was not a clear-cut message from the book. So, instead of using the bumblebee as my focus, I taught on the topic "The Woes of Hurting Women." When I finished my speech, a staff member informed me that my message had been a little bit disappointing. She told me that although she thought my message was helpful to some, it was not the message she wanted me to deliver.

The second conference was just as difficult. I was fearful because I wanted to please the staff at the conference, but I also wanted to do the perfect will of God. I was confused and frustrated. I sought advice and counsel from my administrative assistant, Pat. She reminded me that God had sent His Holy Spirit to dwell inside me as my helper, guide, provider, and comforter, and that He would not give me an assignment I could not handle. Then we prayed together that God would remove my fear, give me a clear message from Him, and help me deliver His message without any apprehension.

Since then, the Holy Spirit has strengthened my message. I incorporate the bumblebee image into my speech as a reference and also seek God's help to give me new inspiration and specific messages for every conference.

At the conference in Phoenix, the Holy Spirit showed me a vision of large holes in the sand with water bubbling from them. The interpretation was one of hope. I spoke of a revival that would begin there because of the faith and influence of Christian women in the area. Ministries would be born and thousands of people from all walks of life would be saved.

In Nashville, following the devastating tornadoes on April 16, 1998, I used the story of how Jesus calmed the winds and the waves as they were raging against the boat carrying Him and His disciples to illustrate how He can calm the waves of sin, doubt, fear, shaky finances, marital woes, sickness, demanding careers, rebellious children, abuse, addiction, homelessness, immorality, low self-esteem, prejudice, oppression, depression, loneliness, codependency, and every other storm that rages in our lives.

People have asked me whether I get nervous talking in front of thousands of people. No, I do not; my desire is always to give a message of joy and hope to others.

God's Enabling Power
When You Need an Answer

Many nights we've prayed
With no proof anyone could hear.

160

In our hearts a hopeful song

We barely understood.

Now we are not afraid

Although we know there's much to fear.

We were moving mountains

Long before we knew we could.

—Miriam, singing "When You Believe" (POE)

As a little girl, I would pray all the time—for God to reveal things to me, for other people, for myself, for everything I could think of. My great-grandparents influenced much of my prayer life. We were praying people. We prayed at every meal. I followed them to prayer meeting on Wednesday nights. My great-grandfather was a deacon in the church and was known as a prayer warrior who would pray for the worship services on Sunday mornings. I even enjoyed playing prayer meeting with my great-grandfather when we were at home. Praying has always been a part of my life.

Playing prayer meeting as a little girl was fun. But as I grew up and began to face real-life situations and challenges, disappointments, trials, tribulations, and heartache, my prayer life changed. As a youngster, I prayed for good grades and studied so that I could get them. I prayed for nice clothes and shoes, and my great-grandmother would get them for me. I prayed for a husband, and I married George when I turned twenty years old. I prayed that I would be a nice girl, and (for the most part) I practiced being nice.

There were so many prayers that God seemed to answer quickly. But with more responsibility as a wife, mother, career woman, community citizen, and church leader, my quickly answered prayers seemed to decrease. God seemed to have stopped listening to me. My experience seemed similar to a story one of my friends told me. She said, "I prayed one prayer in particular for eighteen years with little hope of a solution.

162

"One of my children was addicted to drugs. He had started using marijuana at an early age without our realizing it. He quickly went from one drug to another until he was hooked on crack cocaine.

"How could this be? The child had been raised in church. He went to Sunday school, morning worship, vacation Bible school, and prayer meeting with me. He knew the difference between right and wrong. He had been baptized and had publicly acknowledged Jesus Christ as Lord and Savior. He was shown love and affection from the moment he was born. Even as a teenager, he was involved in church. So how could this be happening to a solid Christian family?"

I guess Moses could have asked a similar question when he saw the pitiful conditions and ill treatment of the Israelites. How could this be happening to God's chosen people? Surely God didn't want His people to live in captivity forever. As Miriam sings in the song "When You Believe," they had spent many nights praying with no proof that anyone could hear. But God was listening. He answered

Moses, saying,

> I have surely seen the oppression of My people who are in
> Egypt, and have heard their cry because of their taskmasters,
> for I know their sorrows. So I have come down to deliver
> them out of the hand of the Egyptians, and to bring them
> up from that land to a good and large land, to a land flow-
> ing with milk and honey, to the place of the Canaanites and
> the Hittites and the Amorites and the Perizzites and the
> Hivites and the Jebusites. (Ex. 3:7–8 NKJV)

Finally the Israelites received the answer they waited many years
to hear. They would be set free.

My friend continued, "I desperately needed to hear God say that
my child would be set free. As his drug habit progressed, it seemed
to swallow the entire family. Family arguments, lying, stealing, and
depression were the order of the day. Some members of the family
went through guilt trips wondering what we had done to cause the
situation. When blaming ourselves did not work, we resorted to
blaming others. Everyone was on an emotional roller-coaster day in
and day out. And I was on my face every morning, noon, and night
praying. As often as I could, for the eighteen years from 1976 until
1994, I asked God for deliverance.

"In my frustration, I asked God for a sign that He was listening:

'Lord, if You are going to heal and deliver this child from drug addiction, please show me by letting him get sick to his stomach and throw up.' A few weeks later, my son asked to borrow the car. Just as he started to drive the car out of the driveway, he got sick to his stomach and started vomiting. A few weeks later he asked to borrow the car again. When he got out of the driveway and down the street, he got sick again. He came stumbling back into the house and said he did not understand what was happening to him. Every time he got in the car he got sick. It happened a third time. He stormed back in to the house, opened the door to my room, and yelled, 'Every time I get in your car I get sick. You must be praying for me. Stop praying for me! Leave me alone! Stop praying for me!'

"Three times the Lord showed me through this sign that my child would be delivered, but He didn't tell me when. I thought He was showing me that deliverance would come soon, so my prayers slacked off a bit. Instead of the addiction getting better, it got worse. More episodes of violence, stealing, lying, and everything that goes with drug addiction occurred over the next several years. I began praying continually again.

"Something began to happen to me as I prayed. Although my child showed little improvement, a peace started to take hold of my spirit. There was a joy in my heart that I could not explain or share with others, for fear that they would not understand. It was joy unspeakable.

"God was empowering me to wait. He would make all things possible in His time. He had not forsaken me or my child. I did not know why I had to wait, but I knew deep down inside that God had heard my prayer and the prayers of other family members.

"While we were waiting, we made some tough decisions as a family. We decided to find out what enablement was and to stop it. We decided to practice tough love—the kind of love that says I love you, but I'm not going to blindly accept your behavior or ill treatment. We had to realize our limitations to change the situation. We learned to pray as a family. We began to study about Satan and how he, the enemy, attacks us at our weakest point. We began to share our feelings openly.

"In 1993, we started seeing a little progress. Our child finally admitted he had a problem and asked for help. It was a beginning. An intervention drug treatment program was finally the option he needed to work through his sickness. But we never stopped praying in spite of the fact that progress was being made."

My friend felt like Miriam, who sings in *The Prince of Egypt*, "Now we are not afraid although we know there's much to fear" (POE). Continuing her story, she explained, "One day I was praying, and the Holy Spirit spoke to me and said, *I have heard your prayers. Stop praying to Me about this. Stop praying and start praising.* I immediately stopped praying and started praising. Each time I thought about praying for the situation, I remembered the Holy Spirit's words. Praising became second nature to me within a few weeks.

"Eight more months went by with some progress, but deep within my heart, I knew that the time was near. In 1994, our son checked into another rehabilitation facility, and that time, came out a free man. God had done His part to heal and deliver. The verse 'Train up a child in the way he should go, and when he is old he will not depart from it' (Prov. 22:6 NKJV), took on a completely different meaning for me. It meant that when you train a child in the ways of the Lord, whatever the child does and wherever the child goes, the Word of God will never leave his memory and God will always be with him.

"My child is now married, has children, and lives a productive Christian life. God gave my family a testimony of His faithfulness."

God did it for the Israelites, just as He will for you. My friend's triumphant story brings hope to us all.

Never give up. Keep praying in faith believing that God has answered your prayers. You may have to wait for several years or generations for the fullness of His answer, but while you're waiting here are some things you can do:

- Study your Bible.

- Pray alone in your secret closet and pray with other believers.

- Think of things that are beautiful, lovely, truthful, and of good report.

- Work for a cause larger than yourself.

- Seek Christian counseling.

- Read inspirational books; watch inspirational television.

167

- Confide in a few Christian friends you can trust.

- Listen to praise music and praise Him in your heart all day every day.

- Keep faith and hope alive, and know that God will work things out for your good.

GOD'S ENABLING POWER WHEN YOU NEED HIM MOST

"Take the staff in your hand, Moses . . . with it you shall do My wonders."
—God, speaking to Moses (POE)

When I was a little girl in the St. John Missionary Baptist Church, I remember the senior choir dressed in their black robes with the tiny white collars singing a cappella the words to this old spiritual: "I'm going to die with the staff in my hand." We would repeat that line, and then one of the choir members would start another line: "My mother died with the staff in her hand." And we'd repeat that line. Then somebody else would add a line: "My father died with the staff in his hand."

We would continue by singing,

Sometimes I'm reeled and I'm rocked from side to side.
I'm going to die, die with the staff in my hand.

Once we finished that song, people would be shouting, crying, raising holy hands, stomping their feet, and dancing or walking the aisles emotionally. In our church we call it getting happy. The church would remain in a state of jubilation and celebration for the rest of the service.

I did not know what in the world we were singing about, it just sounded good to me. Often I wondered, "What is a staff? What are they talking about?"

All the children of the church memorized the Twenty-third Psalm. I didn't have a clue what we were saying when we repeated, "Your rod and Your staff, they comfort me" (NKJV). But I knew when I said it, something on the inside of me felt safe. Today, I understand why I felt safe. I know the meaning of the "rod" and "staff."

The "rod" is a short stick that reminds me of a policeman's club.

It is a weapon used for protection, defense, and discipline. It symbolizes God's strength, might, power, sovereignty, and authority. The "staff" is a slender, straight stick about three to six feet long with a hook on one end. To me, it looks like the tall cane used by my grandfather and some of his friends to help them walk. I actually saw a shepherd holding a staff on the mountain plains of Israel when I visited there some years ago. It represents God's security in a time of need and His pledge to guide us and keep us on the right path.

The rod and the staff are examples of God's genuine love for us and His all-knowing guidance in our lives. They give us the sweet assurance that He is always with us; that we can go through the fires of life and not be burned; that we can go through the rivers of life and not be drowned; that we can go through the valley of the shadow of death and be comforted.

God uses simple, easy-to-understand things to help us realize His power in and through us. When God told Moses to go back to Egypt and tell Pharaoh to "let my people go," Moses became scared. He didn't want to go. He whined, "Suppose they will not believe me or listen to my voice; suppose they say, 'The LORD has not appeared to you.'" Then the Lord said to him, "What is that in your hand?" Moses answered that it was a staff. God told Moses to throw the staff on the ground, and when he did, it became a snake. At the Lord's instruction, Moses reached out and took hold of the snake. Suddenly it turned into a staff in his hand. "This," said the

Lord, "is so that they may believe that the LORD God of their fathers, the God of Abraham, the God of Isaac, and the God of Jacob, has appeared to you" (Ex. 4:1–5 NKJV).

God took an ordinary stick and used it to teach Moses a valuable lesson. That He, the Lord God almighty, would provide Moses with everything he needed to do the task God had assigned him to do. God never gives us more than we can bear. He never leaves us without all the resources, equipment, knowledge, wisdom, ability, talent, skill, protection, guidance, and provisions to perform His assignments well.

170

During 1997 and 1998, I spoke to several religious organizations whose members did not believe in Jesus Christ as the Messiah and Savior of the world. I wondered why I was asked to speak for them. Why didn't they get someone who believed as they believed? As I prepared for the first engagement, I was frightened about what to say and how to say it. But the closer the speaking time came, the more clearly I understood what I should say. I prayed and asked God for help and strength. He gave me the wisdom to address them this way: "I greet you in the name of Jehovah God, the Creator, and in the name of Jeshua, my Messiah and Savior." There was a stillness in the room that you could have cut with a knife. But it didn't matter to me because I had the staff of salvation and the Holy Spirit operating with me. Continuing the message, I made a number of references to how Jesus was working in my life. Before I knew it several people shouted words such as, "Speak, sister!" "Say that, sister." "Right on." "Yes!" God's rod and staff, the symbols of God's protection, love, and guidance, were lifted up in what the Holy Spirit was saying through me. People were changed and liberated.

God can take the ordinary things we take for granted and perform miraculous signs. He can take a singer's voice, a musician's instrument, a writer's pen, a speaker's words, a leader's ability, a parent's good example, a child's innocence, a wealthy person's resources, a poor person's kindness, a younger person's vitality, an older person's wisdom, a teachable person's openness, a cheerful person's smile, a caretaker's humanity, a faith-filled person's prayers, a hopeful person's excitement, an available person's willingness, a hard worker's tenacity, a patient person's perseverance, a happy person's joy, and a righteous person's lifestyle to release a people and a world from the bonds of the enemy. And all the pharaohs throughout the generations cannot stand against God's plans.

That's what God was saying to Moses when he said, "So I will stretch out My hand and strike Egypt with all My wonders which I will do in its midst; and after that he will let you go. And I will give this people favor in the sight of the Egyptians; and it shall be, when you go, that you shall not go empty-handed" (Ex. 3:20–21 NKJV).

It is amazing to think we have the love of God, the salvation of Jesus, and the guidance and protection of the Holy Spirit with us every minute of every day, every week of every month, and every month of every year in our lives. Everything we need is available to us. All we have to do is raise our rod.

Moses raised his staff, and the Red Sea was parted so that the children of Israel could safely make it to the other side. We all have Red Seas. Sometimes they are Red Seas of finance, heartache, shame, guilt, danger, homelessness, separation of loved ones, pressure from society or job, relationships, children, spouse or lack thereof, health and disease, abuse and abusing, poverty (even wealth), loneliness, incompetence, addiction, abandonment, hunger, and helplessness—anything that causes you pain in your being. But there is safety in the staff of Jesus. There is hope in the staff of Jesus.

172

I now understand what the old saints in my church were singing about when they sang, "I'm going to die with the staff in my hand." They meant that, without a doubt, God would meet their every need. God would never forsake them and never let them down. God was on their side. What joy! What peace! What assurance!

God uses ordinary people to help Him fulfill His kingdom on earth. He took Moses—a refugee from Egypt, a murderer, a sheepherder, a slave by his ancestry, a man with a speech impediment—and equipped him with everything it took to lead his people to freedom.

God took me—a poor, illegitimate girl of slave ancestry—and enabled me to defy the odds. Through His power, I am a witness to millions of people worldwide. This is a message for you. It is one of hope that God cares for you. He will give you faith, courage, commitment, and extraordinary abilities to accomplish your mission in Jesus Christ. My, my! God makes ordinary people extraordinary.

173

MOSES, PRINCE OF ISRAEL

PHILIP YANCEY

*In this essay, Philip Yancey examines
Moses' experiences with God and the children
of Israel from Moses' perspective
at the end of his life. Yancey observes
that although evil is unpreventable and
punishment inevitable, we have a God of
grace who consciously forgets our sins and
consciously remembers our frailty.*

MOSES,

PRINCE OF ISRAEL

hen Communism fell in 1989, small countries in Eastern Europe and Central Asia suddenly found themselves free of the long shadow of the Soviet Union. No one gave them orders anymore. No one imposed policies. On their own they had to figure out how to design a flag, train an army, decide foreign affairs, settle border disputes—in short, how to run a country. Each nation's success or failure depended on what kind of leader emerged from the Cold War thaw.

Czechoslovakia instinctively turned to Vaclav Havel, a playwright who had spent years in prison for his political dissent. Although Havel had no experience and little interest in politics, he accepted the daunting task of fashioning a new country. To connect with his people, he began a practice that became a tradition: each week he appeared on television to answer callers' questions. He explained how the new government would work, went over the budget, discussed controversial new laws, lectured on morality and responsibility. At times preacher, cheerleader, historian, and coach, this playwright-intellectual against all odds became a media star, presiding over one of the most popular shows in the country. By sheer eloquence and force of personality Havel ushered the Czech people through a painful split with Slovakia and prepared them for life as an independent nation. It felt, he said, like a parent trying to teach an unruly bunch of children how to behave as adults.

In a nutshell, that is the situation Moses confronted toward the end of his life. The movie *The Prince of Egypt* covers the beginning of his story. A reluctant leader who had just spent forty years tending sheep in a wilderness, he was abruptly called by God to emancipate the Hebrews from the most powerful empire in the world. Moses did that and more, coaxing and cajoling the freed slaves through four decades of immaturity in the Sinai Desert. And now, just as Moses' own life was ending, the Hebrews stood at the threshold of the promised land, eager to take the reins of nationhood. Now Moses had one last shot, one last opportunity to pass along historical memory, to purge himself of grievances and pain, to bequeath to them the hope and spirit they would desperately need in his absence. To his people, he represented not only a trailblazer like Vaclav Havel; he was the Liberator—Simon Bolivar, Mahatma Gandhi, George Washington, and Abraham Lincoln all pressed into one frail old body.

"If the various writers of the Bible were composers, the Deuteronomist would be Bach in his utter, majestic confidence," writes Jack Miles. Deuteronomy is the last of the five "books of Moses," the grand summation, the first full-blown oratory in the Bible, and the record of Moses' final words to the children of Israel. In forty torturous years a stuttering shepherd, shy of leadership and haunted by his own crimes of passion, had become one of the giants of history whose achievements would change the planet forever. Moses Prince of Egypt had developed into Moses Prince of Israel. The film *The Prince of Egypt* presents his character and destiny as they develop through the Exodus, but these events only begin his remarkable transformation, which Moses recounts in Deuteronomy.

179

The old man clutches his robe and shivers in spite of the desert heat. Assistants help him scrabble up the tallest rock. Before him, stretching all the way to the horizon, are the Israelites. He pauses to let the cheers of the crowd die down. His eyes lock onto a few anonymous faces. So young, so innocent. None of them has a single memory of the glories of Egypt, the fabulous land of pyramids and palaces and chariots. These desert kids know only the rigors of Sinai: scorpions, vipers, blazing heat, cold nights, sandstorms, the endless search for water.

Like a hive of bees, the mob buzzes with energy. Moses hasn't seen such excitement since the day their parents walked out of Egypt. How quickly the smiles left their faces; how long will they last on these children's? They have heard stories from their parents, he knows—the same parents who grumbled, complained, and sometimes rebelled against his leadership.

180

This is his last chance to set the record straight, to get history down not just for these children but for all to follow, for all posterity.

Moses' eyes, covered with cataracts, are the color of clotted milk. Eighty years in the desert have carved walrus wrinkles across his face. He can barely hear; the sounds of the multitude blend together into a low hum. Joshua and Caleb, trusted associates, have quieted the throng and are motioning for him to begin. They've arranged for "shouters" to repeat his words, projecting them out so everyone can hear. "Speak slowly," they tell him. "Take your time." But as he begins to speak, his voice cracks and the old stutter starts up again.

Moses is the oldest person any of the Israelites have seen, the only truly ancient person among them, nearly twice the age of Joshua and Caleb. With his snow-white hair and flowing beard, he seems more mythological creature than man. He has dominated their lives from birth. They have heard how he strode past guards in the great Pharaoh's palace and surprised the ruler who was once his playmate. The plagues, so traumatic at the time, over the years have become the fodder of jokes: frogs jumping through the kitchen, gnats and flies swarming the soldiers and foremen, boils forcing the Egyptian magicians to roll naked in the sand for relief.

Their parents used to speak longingly of the palm trees, the houses piled atop one another so high as to block the sun, the streets crowded with chariots, donkey carts, and long caravans of camels. Of such they have no memory. They have only the hope of a new start, a nation where they will serve as masters and not slaves, a land not desiccated but lush with pastures and crops, a land they can call their own.

*Indented, italicized passages are adapted from the HOLY BIBLE: NEW INTERNATIONAL VERSION.

From the beginning, Moses' life had a single theme: God did it. How many times had his mother recounted the tale of his miraculous survival during the pharaoh's campaign against Hebrew infants? "God saved you, Moses," she told him over and over. "He has a very special plan for you." Meanwhile he played in the courts of Pharaoh, raced chariots with his brother and best friend, acquired a superb classical education, and dined with the elite of the empire.

181

As he faced his true identity, Moses felt like a person without a country. Among his own people, he was taunted for his uppity manners and palace accent. He loved both families, birth and adopted. He never tired of the peasant feasts of the Hebrews, followed by the old men recounting tales of Abraham, Isaac, and Jacob and the God they still worshiped.

On the other hand, he could not imagine life without the education he was getting every day with the smartest students in the empire. Nor could he imagine life without sports, especially the fierce rivalry with his best friend, the pharaoh's son. He loved the feasts, the fine wine, the oiled and perfumed women who taught him art and music. Like a spy, he balanced the two worlds successfully, keeping them in sealed compartments, flourishing in both—until one day the two worlds collided and he had to make a choice.

Dressed in the full regalia of an Egyptian prince, a gold headpiece and buckle announcing his office, he was visiting a work site of the pharaoh. There he saw a mid-level Egyptian foreman beating a Hebrew, one of Moses' countrymen. Unable to watch passively, he gave the tyrant a shove and finished him off.

To Pharaoh, Moses had crossed a line and got caught on the wrong side. "They're only slaves," that Pharaoh once said about the Hebrews. It was he, after all, who had ordered the infanticide campaign that exterminated much of Moses' generation. "Sometimes for the greater good, sacrifices must be made" (POE). On that day at the work site, Moses realized what side he was truly on. Egyptians used the word *Hapiru* as a term of scorn for Hebrews: "the dusty ones." If an Egyptian dies, of course someone must pay. But if one of the Hapiru dies, who cares? I care, Moses decided. They may be slaves, but they are my kinsmen. No one deserves this treatment.

A fugitive, Moses fled Egypt and for forty years had no contact with either of his families. A new life began that surprisingly suited him, the lonely life of a nomad. He gained a wife, an extended family, and a new set of wilderness survival skills. His world gradually shrank into a circle of domestic tranquillity, and at the ripe old age of eighty he concerned himself mainly with children, in-laws, and sheep.

God, however, had other plans. While Moses had been forging a new life in Midian, far from the Hebrew slaves, God had been listening to their groans. All at once, the slow, mysterious work of a timeless God became clear: nothing in Moses' circuitous life had been wasted. God now had a Hebrew of pure pedigree, expertly trained in Egyptian leadership skills, fully capable of surviving in the wilderness. The time for liberation of God's chosen people had arrived. Now to convince Moses. And Pharaoh.

Moses raised powerful objections. First, there was the question of his trustworthiness. Why should the Hebrews trust someone trained by the enemy who had skipped the country for forty years? And both the Hebrews and Pharaoh would need an articulate leader to stir them into action—why pick someone with a stutter? "O Lord, please send someone else" (Ex. 4:13 NIV), Moses begged. God's words spoken from the burning bush silenced Moses; convincing Pharaoh was another matter.

Thus did a diffident shepherd become the first intermediary chosen by God to speak to His people, and also the first person recorded in the Bible to work miracles. Moses' initial fears, however, proved accurate. Upon his return to Egypt, Moses did not even have the support of his own people as he strode up the massive stone steps to Pharaoh's palace, its gold finials gleaming in the desert sun.

Moses looked around. As the movie *The Prince of Egypt* illustrates so well, the pharaoh had nearly finished his grand construction plans. A "city of white limestone, more dazzling than the sun" (POE) had grown up around the buildings he knew as a boy.

The wilderness of Midian had rid him of all nostalgia for the luxuries of Egypt. He knew his proper identity now: a foreigner, an alien in a strange land, a *Gershom*, the very name he had chosen for his son. His people, the Hebrews, were suffering: the Hapiru, the dusty ones who worked in the mud and bore the lashes of the Egyptians. Their only hope, only future, now rested in God's hands alone.

To the Egyptians, the Hebrews' notion of a single, invisible God seemed ludicrous. They worshiped an elaboration of animate gods who could be visually celebrated in the splendid temples: Horus the hawk, Thot the ibis, Khunm the ram, Apis the sacred bull. Each possessed mysterious characteristics known only to the priests. What good was a god you could not see, or even represent in sculpture or painting?

184

Why on earth would my appointment secretary admit this smelly goatherd? thought Pharaoh on seeing but not yet recognizing Moses.

A few minutes later Moses the former prince of Egypt and Pharaoh the ruling king were laughing together over the good old days when they were known throughout the palace as adolescent terrors. The pharaoh's gold necklaces and bracelets rattled as he clapped his hands in joy.

Anything Moses wanted, he could have—for himself only, that is, not for the rest of the Hebrews. Though the pharaoh did not say it, they both knew the Hebrew slaves were essential: they did all the dirty work, at minimal cost. "I have to maintain the ancient traditions," he said. "I bear the weight of my father's crown" (POE).

God had not forgotten the Hebrews, however: "I have seen the oppression of my people in Egypt and have heard their cry," He told

Moses from the burning bush (POE). And neither could Moses forget his people. He looked back in shame on the days when he called "Father" the man who had slaughtered the Hebrew children. After forty years in the wilderness, he had been unprepared for the sight of slave labor again. It felt like a kick in the gut. "No kingdom, however glorious, should be built on the backs of slaves!" he declared, in effect flinging down a gauntlet before the pharaoh (POE).

Soon Moses and the pharaoh were engaged in a great tug-of-war, not so different from the games they used to play in the courtyards although now with stakes much higher. "I will not be dictated to! I will not be threatened!" shouted the pharaoh in a tone Moses had never before heard. "I am the morning and the evening star. I am Pharaoh!" (POE).

Moses, who more than once left those palace meetings hot with anger, had challenged the mightiest empire in the world to a form of single-warrior combat, with the very heavens choosing sides. Egypt and its mighty gods stood in splendid array against the invisible God of the Hebrews. "You're playing with the big boys now," the Egyptian priests taunted Moses (POE). Yes, but eye had not yet seen the power of the One the big boys were about to face.

One by one, the Egyptian gods fell to the plagues unleashed by Moses' God: the river god turned to blood, the sacred fly became a swarming pest, the sun-god Ra disappeared behind a cloud, the great bull failed to protect his livestock. Finally, in the last and worst plague the pharaoh, along with every other Egyptian, lost his first-born son. At last he conceded defeat; the invisible God had won. And the very next day Hebrew slaves, loaded down with Egyptian plunder, walked away in a huge, ragtag mob, at the head of which marched Moses, Prince of Israel.

Moses himself would have resisted the title, of course. From the moment he first saw the bush that would not stop burning, he had learned one lesson above all others: the mission was God's, not his. Moses merely played the role God assigned him. He tried to drum that lesson into the Israelites every year at Passover, when they remembered that last, murderous night in Egypt. No Israelite armies faced the mighty Egyptians. Freedom came in the blackest night while Hebrew families huddled around the Passover table, their bags packed, waiting for deliverance. God alone did it. Later, when the pharaoh changed his mind and set his chariots loose upon the fleeing tribes, and all the Israelites whimpered like cowards, God came through again. God even designated the Exodus as a way of describing himself: "I am the God who brought you out of Egypt."

That same pattern of abject dependence would continue all through the wilderness wanderings. When the Hebrews ran out of water, God provided. When food supplies failed, God provided. When raiders attacked, God provided. Liberation was God's act, and He alone deserved the credit.

Years of sheepherding during his exile in Midian had mellowed

186

Moses, preparing him for his leadership role in the Sinai. In the old days he took matters into his own hands: murdering an Egyptian foreman, breaking up a fight among his brethren, chasing a bunch of shepherds away from some vulnerable women (and impressing his future wife in the process). Now the famous temper had softened. Once only did it rear up strong enough to defy God Himself: when Moses smashed his walking stick against a rock in anger. "You want water? I'll give you water!" he had screamed at the thirsty whiners. That lapse cost him the dream of his life, the chance to set foot in the promised land. For a moment Moses forgot it was God's work, not his own, and for this reason he at last stands on the tall rock before the anxious multitude on the wrong side of the Jordan River.

187

Keep it positive, old man, he mumbles to himself. Remember, this is their big day. Don't take it away from them. It's their parents who angered God, not these kids here today. Give them hope. Let them celebrate.

But try as he might, he cannot help lashing out. Footsore and weary, as he thinks back over the last third of his life, most of what he feels is disappointment. "You are too heavy a burden for me to carry alone," he says, and waits for the shouters to repeat it. Well, it's true, they are a burden.

They're stubborn, like the ox that used to resist his yoking in Midian. Unless the stupid beast relaxed, he could never get the yoke to settle tight across its neck. The ox wore sores all day because of its own stubbornness. This tribe has been wandering for forty years in a wilderness with a yoke bouncing up and down their stiff necks. It should have taken eleven days, this miserable journey, not forty years.

The worst part of all: "Because of you the Lord became angry with me also and said, 'You shall not enter it, either.'" That's what really sticks in his craw. How come these kids get to prance into the land of milk and honey while the great liberator, the one who bore them like a burden, who stuck up for them when even God abandoned them, has to stand at the very edge of happiness . . . and die. It's not fair. None of it is fair. "I told you, but you would not listen. You rebelled against the Lord's command . . ."

The speech is not going well. Moses can sense it in the crowd: the women talking among themselves, the men looking down and shuffling their feet, the children drifting off to play. This is his last shot, and he's blowing it. Still, doesn't he have a right to his say? Hasn't he earned it? Who cares how they respond right now. They've got to listen. One day they'll understand. One day they'll know how much they hurt me.

It was a long speech Moses gave, three speeches in all, and despite his tendency to lapse into rancor against his own ill fortune, he did pull himself together enough to get across the main message, which could be summarized in one word: Remember! With the speeches in Deuteronomy, Moses established the great tradition of historical memory, a tradition that his people, who became known as the Jews, have cherished ever since. "Never forget" is the one redemptive lesson that survived Auschwitz. Try as we might, we can never undo the past, but we must honor it by bearing witness, by remembering so as not to allow it to repeat.

One would think in view of all that had transpired—the centuries of slavery, the Ten Plagues, the Red Sea miracle, the victories over surrounding tribes—the Hebrews would not need such a pedantic reminder. Forget God one generation after the Exodus? How could they ever again doubt such a God? Yet Moses knew by intuition that the simple act of remembering would require daily acts of concentration.

For the LORD your God is bringing you into a good land—a land with streams and pools of water, with springs flowing in the valleys and hills; a land with wheat and barley, vines and fig trees, pomegranates, olive oil and honey; a land where bread will not be scarce and you will lack nothing; a land where the rocks are iron and you can dig copper out of the hills.

When you have eaten and are satisfied, praise the LORD your God for the good land he has given you. Be careful that you do not forget the LORD your God, failing to observe his commands, his laws and his decrees that I am giving you this day. Otherwise, when you eat and are satisfied, when you build fine houses and settle down, and when your herds and flocks grow large and your silver and gold increase and all you have is multiplied, then your heart will become proud and you will forget the LORD your God, who brought you out of Egypt, out of the land of slavery. He led you through the vast and dreadful desert, that thirsty and waterless land, with its venomous snakes and scorpions. He brought you water out of hard rock. He gave you manna to eat in the desert, something your fathers had never known, to humble and to test you so that in the end it might go well with you. You may say to yourself, "My power and the strength of my hands have produced this wealth for me." But remember the LORD your God, for it is he who gives you the ability to produce wealth, and so confirms his covenant, which he swore to your forefathers, as it is today. (Deut. 8:7–18 NIV)

190

These commandments that I give you today are to be upon your hearts. Impress them on your children. Talk about them when you sit at home and when you walk along the road, when you lie down and when you get up. Tie them as symbols on your hands and bind them on your foreheads. Write them on the doorframes of your houses and on your gates.

When the LORD your God brings you into the land he swore to your fathers, to Abraham, Isaac and Jacob, to give you—a land with large, flourishing cities you did not build, houses filled with all kinds of good things you did not provide, wells you did not dig, and vineyards and olive groves you did not plant—then when you eat and are satisfied, be careful that you do not forget the LORD, who brought you out of Egypt, out of the land of slavery. (Deut. 6:6–12 NIV)

191

To underscore his lesson, Moses proceeded to inaugurate a series of feasts to assist the process of remembering. At Passover, the anniversary of their departure from Egypt, the Hebrews must relive that dreadful night in Egypt, eating the same food and bitter herbs, reciting the old stories, remembering the act of liberation. Seven weeks later they must stop work, invite in aliens, widows, and the fatherless, then celebrate another feast with an offering of thanksgiving to the God who had made such bounty possible. Finally, when harvesttime came each fall and produce and grapes filled the storerooms, they must camp out in tents for a week, remembering the days of wandering in the Sinai wilderness.

Success, not failure, is the greatest danger facing any follower of God, as Moses knew well. He had traipsed around a desert for forty years as a penalty for the Hebrews' inability to handle the success of the Exodus. Every significant downfall in his own life had come when he seized power for himself—killing an Egyptian, smashing a rock in the desert—rather than relying on God. In contrast, perhaps his greatest military victory had come when he played an almost slapstick role. No general at the head of his troops, Moses stood apart, atop a nearby hill. As long as he held up his hands toward God, the Israelites won; whenever his hands sank down, the Amalekites won. By the end of the day an exhausted Moses was sitting on a rock with each upstretched arm supported by a helper. God's strength is perfected in weakness.

192

Somehow just talking about the bitterness softens it a little. There have surely been good times, Moses reminds himself. He's had God by his side each step of the way, and even when it feels as though God alone supports him, that is enough.

Once Moses overheard someone talking about "the meekest man on the face of the earth," and to his astonishment he learned they were talking about him! His mother and Pharaoh would certainly never have used that description. Moses chuckles to himself. Probably not God either. Meek? Humble? Imagine.

Over the years Moses has learned something so sweet and strange and mysterious that only one word can begin to capture it: grace, *God's free, undeserved gift. He has learned that God loves him despite his failures, with a pure, stubborn, everlasting love. After more than a century of life, Moses has given up trying to figure out what God sees in him. Or sees in the rest of the Hebrews for that matter. He just accepts it, and gives thanks.*

Moses takes a long draught of water from a goatskin bag, moistens his lips, clears the phlegm from his throat. "Listen up. Pay attention. Here's what I want you to remember. Even if you forget everything else I say, think on this." Another pause, another swallow. The crowd stills, detecting the change in intensity in Moses' voice. An expression of bliss crosses his face so that it almost glows. They know that expression; they've seen it whenever Moses emerges from the sacred tent after his meetings with God.

"The Lord did not set his affection on you and choose you because you were more numerous than other peoples, for you were the fewest of all peoples. But it was because the Lord loved you and kept the oath he swore to your forefathers that he brought you out with a mighty hand and redeemed you from the land of slavery, from the power of Pharaoh king of Egypt. Know therefore that the Lord your God is God; he is the faithful God, keeping his covenant of love to a thousand generations of those who love him and keep his commands."

He is warming to the message now, his weary voice ascending in both pitch and volume.

"To the Lord your God belong the heavens, even the highest heavens, the earth and everything in it. Yet the Lord set his affection on your forefathers and loved them, and he chose you, their descendants, above all the nations, as it is today . . . He is your praise; he is your God, who performed for you those great and awesome wonders you saw with your own eyes. Your forefathers who went down into Egypt were seventy in all, and now the Lord your God has made you as numerous as the stars in the sky."

He drinks again from the goatskin bag, letting the words sink in.

They are responding to the positive tone. Who doesn't want to hear that God loves them? The first time Moses encountered God up close it took his breath away. He hid his face in shame and fear. Yet after forty years of such encounters, he and God have grown to be—could he say it?— friends. He argues with God, even bargains with Him. He loses some-times, as with his request to enter the promised land, but sometimes he wins, like the time God nearly called off the whole project.

194

Moses ignores his notes and begins to ramble, reminding the crowd of that, his finest hour. After three days' journey they had complained about the water; a month later they forgot all about the bullwhips and were mewling about Egypt's figs and pomegranates; then, a month after that, the holiest moment in Moses' life, he descended from the cloud to find a scene that made him retch. He had been meeting with God on the sacred mountain, getting the stone tablets inscribed by God's own hand. When he came down, his face shining like a lantern, he found them cavorting around a golden calf, an Egyptian idol. It was too much.

Though reared among the Egyptians and their animal-shaped gods, Moses rediscovered a fundamental fact about God forgotten during the four hundred years of silence: God is a person. During the years of silence the Hebrews thought of God, if at all, as a distant, unapproachable, ineffable mystery who showed little concern over what was transpiring on earth. Moses proved that you can hardly go wrong "personalizing" God.

God feels pain. When jilted, He hurts like any wounded lover. He meets in a tent and discusses policy, as a man speaks to a friend. He listens, and He argues back. He backs down from threats. He negotiates and signs contracts.

This last fact, above all, separated the Hebrews from their neighbors. Even the haughty Egyptians lived in fear of their capricious gods. The Canaanites sacrificed children to appease their unpredictable gods. But the God of the Hebrews proved willing to sign a contract detailing exactly what He expected from His people, and what He promised in return.

Except for Orthodox Jews, not many people today devote time to the legal code recorded in Exodus, Leviticus, and Deuteronomy. The laws seem repetitious and often irrelevant to modern society. Yet, as Deuteronomy shows most clearly, these laws simply set the boundaries of a vastly unequal relationship: between an awesome, holy God and an ordinary people prone to failure and rebellion.

Moses prefaced the contract with two questions: "What other nation is so great as to have their gods near them the way the LORD our God is near us whenever we pray to Him? And what other nation is so great as to have such righteous decrees and laws as this body of laws I am setting before you today?" (Deut. 6:7–8 NIV).

From there he proceeded to give the Ten Commandments as a reasonable understanding between two parties. For example, "You saw no form of any kind the day the LORD spoke to you at Horeb out of the fire" (Deut. 4:15 NIV); so why fashion idols in the shape of a man or woman or animal? Each command grew out of their unique relationship with God.

Years later, Moses knew, some would question specific laws in the contract. Moses anticipated such a question:

> In the future, when your son asks you, "What is the meaning of the stipulations, decrees and laws the LORD our God has commanded you?" tell him: "We were slaves of Pharaoh in Egypt, but the LORD brought us out of Egypt with a mighty hand. Before our eyes the LORD sent miraculous signs and wonders—great and terrible—upon Egypt and Pharaoh and his whole household. But he brought us out from there to bring us in and give us the land that he promised on oath to our forefathers. The LORD commanded us to obey all these decrees and to fear the LORD our God, so that we might always prosper and be kept alive, as is the case today. And if we are careful to obey all this law before the LORD our God, as he has commanded us, that will be our righteousness." (Deut. 6:20–25 NIV)

In short, God gave the laws for the Hebrews' own good. Their prosperity, their very survival depended on this contract. Moses spelled out God's end of the bargain in vivid detail. Israelite wives would have many babies. All their crops would produce bountifully. Cattle and sheep would multiply. He even included this extraordinary promise: "The LORD will keep you free from every disease" (Deut. 7:15 NIV). For the Israelites to receive these benefits, God asked only one thing in return—a big thing, as it turned out: follow the covenant agreement set forth in the contract.

God had an unprecedented relationship with the band of refugees who had been roaming the Sinai for forty years. Moses, for one, could not seem to get over it: "Ask from one end of the heavens to the other. Has anything so great as this ever happened, or has anything like it ever been heard of? . . . Has any god ever tried to take for himself one nation out of another nation . . . like . . . the LORD your God did for you in Egypt before your very eyes?" (Deut. 4:32, 34 NIV).

Now, at this moment, the wondrous plan was being fulfilled. God the sovereign chooser, the steadfast promise-maker, was bringing His chosen people into the promised land.

Moses' voice is tiring. He pauses more and more frequently. There is so little energy left, so little time. When he began the speech, he had the feeling he could stave off death by talking. Now he hardly cares. Fatigue has numbed life. He has said it all and more, rambling, repeating, breaking down in tears in all the wrong places.

What, really, will they remember? Scribes are writing down the words for posterity, but against the enemies the Hebrews will soon meet, words make frail allies.

An idea. Back in Egypt they used stones for monuments. On columns, obelisks, and rock walls they wrote of Pharaoh's exploits and recorded the laws of the empire. When a criminal pled ignorance, they merely dragged him to the stone and pointed to the law he had broken. What if the Hebrews do that?

198

"Do it!" Moses commands. "When you have crossed the Jordan into the land the Lord your God is giving you, set up some large stones and coat them with plaster. Write on them all the words of this law . . . And when you have crossed the Jordan, set up these stones on Mount Ebal, as I command you today, and coat them with plaster."

A start, at least. What else? How can he impress on these people the meaning of a contract with God Almighty? More ideas. Moses assigns the tribe of Levites to shout out the laws. "Cursed is the man who moves his neighbor's boundary stone," they yell. Then all the people must say, "Amen!" so they'll have no excuse. *Make them ratify this covenant point by point, aloud.*

Next Moses appoints two antiphonal "choirs." They carry no melody but the discordant tones of the words they shout. Across the Jordan River, two mountains form a natural amphitheater. On Mount Gerizim six tribes of "optimists" will stand to recite the blessings.

"The Lord will grant that the enemies who rise up against you will be defeated before you. They will come at you from one direction but flee from you in seven.

"The Lord will open the heavens, the storehouse of his bounty, to send rain on your land in season and to bless all the work of your hands. You will lend to many nations but will borrow from none. The Lord will make you the head, not the tail. If you pay attention to the commands of the Lord your God that I give you this day and carefully follow them, you will always be at the top, never at the bottom."

More assurances along that line: victory in war, good weather, a boom economy, health, prosperity. Every leader promises such, of course, but in this case God Himself has signed the contract.

Knowing these people, they'll need some warnings as well.

"The Lord will strike you with wasting disease, with fever and inflammation, with scorching heat and drought, with blight and mildew, which will plague you until you perish. The sky over your head will be bronze, the ground beneath you iron. The Lord will turn the rain of your country into dust and powder; it will come down from the skies until you are destroyed.

"The Lord will cause you to be defeated before your enemies . . . The Lord will afflict you with the boils of Egypt and with tumors . . . from which you cannot be cured. The Lord will afflict you with madness, blindness and confusion of mind. At midday you will grope about like a blind man in the dark. You will be unsuccessful in everything you do; day after day you will be oppressed and robbed, with no one to rescue you."

God, could it be? Could You possibly abandon your people like this? Moses sees it so clearly it makes his knees sag and his heart skip beats. But

199

he can hardly believe these things will happen to the people God loves.

"All these curses will come upon you . . . Because you did not serve the Lord your God joyfully and gladly in the time of prosperity, therefore in hunger and thirst, in nakedness and dire poverty, you will serve the enemies the Lord sends against you."

He sees the enemy siege as if it is happening before him. He sees the piles of bodies, the parents fighting over their children's corpses, the beautiful Jewish maidens turned into haggard witches. Oh, if only his eyes would fail and spare him this sight. If only the Hebrews would go deaf and not hear these curses. But they must, they must. Knowing is their only chance of preventing.

200

"You who were as numerous as the stars in the sky will be left but few in number, because you did not obey the Lord your God. Just as it pleased the Lord to make you prosper and increase in number, so it will please him to ruin and destroy you. You will be uprooted from the land you are entering to possess.

"Then the Lord will scatter you among all nations, from one end of the earth to the other . . . There the Lord will give you an anxious mind, eyes weary with longing, and a despairing heart. You will live in constant suspense, filled with dread both night and day, never sure of your life. In the morning you will say, 'If only it were evening!' and in the evening, 'If only it were morning!'—because of the terror that will fill your hearts and the sights that your eyes will see. The Lord will send you back in ships to Egypt on a journey I said you should never make again. There you will *offer yourselves for sale to your enemies as male and female slaves, but no one will buy you."*

Moses cannot go on. What else can he say? A horror grips him as he sounds the words: the horror of truth. His voice has fallen to a whisper. What he delivers as dire warnings to keep his people from sin are, he knows, direct prophecies.

"See, I set before you today life and prosperity, death and destruction," Moses cries into the air that has grown suddenly still. "This day I call heaven and earth as witness against you that I have set before you life and death, blessings and curses. Now choose life! For the Lord is your life."

201

Spent, voiceless, the tottery old man collapses into the arms of his assistants, and no one in that vast throng makes a sound as they gently hand him down from the rock to others waiting on the ground.

More than anything, God longed for the covenant with the Hebrews to succeed: "Oh, that their hearts would be inclined to fear me and keep all my commands always, so that it might go well with them and their children forever!" (Deut. 5:29 NIV), He told Moses. But the repeated rebellions in the wilderness took their toll. Although the movie *The Prince of Egypt* ends with triumph and hope, any sequel would need to detail renewed suffering and despair. After Sinai even God spoke of the future with a tone of resignation approaching fatalism, like the parent of a drug addict helpless to stop his own child from self-destructing.

Two staged memory lessons were not enough. Despite Moses' exhausted state, God required one more assignment of him, a very odd assignment indeed. Write down a song, God said, and make the Israelites learn it as a witness to history. It is one thing to read laws written on stone and plaster, or to hear curses and blessings broadcast from the mountaintops—these sights, these sounds will fade away. Make them, every one of them, learn My words by heart. Drill the message inside them.

The song that appears in Deuteronomy 32 set to music God's own point of view: the story of a parent grieved to the point of desertion. Thus at the birth of their nation, euphoric over the crossing of the Jordan River, the Israelites premiered a kind of national anthem, the strangest national anthem that has ever been sung.

They sang first of the favored times, when God found them in a howling wasteland, and treasured them as the apple of His eye. They sang of the awful betrayal to come, when they would forget the God who gave them birth. They sang of the curses that would afflict them, the wasting famine, deadly plague, and arrows slick with blood. With this bittersweet music ringing in their ears, they marched into the promised land.

"I have been to the mountaintop," said Martin Luther King Jr. in his final speech, making a haunting allusion to Moses. "[God's] allowed me to go up to the mountain, and I've looked over, and I've seen the promised land. I may not get there with you. But I want you to know tonight that we, as a people, will get to the promised land. And so I'm happy tonight . . . Mine eyes have seen the glory of the coming of the Lord." After that speech King returned to his motel room, was hit by an assassin's bullet, and died in a pool of blood.

On the same day that Moses taught the Israelites the melancholy song of their future, he climbed Mount Nebo, squinted against the sun, and gazed in every direction as far as he could see. He had climbed the mountain. He had seen the promised land. And there at its frontier, Moses died.

203

Deuteronomy adds this eulogy: "Since then, no prophet has risen in Israel like Moses, whom the LORD knew face to face, who did all those miraculous signs and wonders the LORD sent him to do in Egypt—to Pharaoh and to all his officials and to his whole land. For no one has ever shown the mighty power or performed the awesome deeds that Moses did in the sight of all Israel" (Deut. 34:10–12 NIV).

He was their preacher, historian, soldier, prophet, judge, politician, priest. Centuries later another Jewish writer, Elie Wiesel, elaborated on Moses' contribution:

Moses, the most solitary and most powerful hero in Biblical history. The immensity of his task and the scope of his experience command our admiration, our reverence, our awe. Moses, the man who changed the course of his-

tory all by himself; his emergence became the decisive turning point. After him, nothing was the same again.

It is not surprising that he occupies a special place in the
Jewish tradition. His passion for social justice, his struggle
for national liberation, his triumphs and disappointments,
his poetic inspiration, his gifts as a strategist and his orga-
nizational genius, his complex relationship with God and
His people, his requirements and promises, his condemna-
tions and blessing, his bursts of anger, his silences, his
efforts to reconcile the law with compassion, authority
with integrity—no individual, ever, anywhere, accomplished so much for so many people in so many different
domains. His influence is boundless, it reverberates beyond
time. The Law bears his name, the Talmud is but its com-
mentary and Kabbala communicates only its silence.

After Moses, nothing was the same again. One man came to
stand for his people, and with good reason. Adopted by an imperi-
al parent, punished for his rashness, sentenced to wander forty years
in the wilderness, forgiven, restored, hand-selected for an impossible
task, accompanied by the overwhelming presence of God at every
step—Moses' personal history replays, in miniature, the history of
his people.

Others have borrowed parts of Moses' message, but none have

quite gotten it all. Liberationists of all stripes, from Marxists to American slaves to base communities in Latin America, have appropriated the language of Exodus, yet all lack Moses' unstinting realism. They drift into utopian promises of a promised land that has never been and will never be:

O Canaan, sweet Canaan,
I am bound for the land of Canaan.

Gonna lay down my sword and shield,
Down by the riverside,
I ain't gonna study war no more.

Pietist Christians have also borrowed Moses' language to describe a victorious Christian life on the other side of the Jordan River.

On Jordan's stormy banks I stand,
And cast a wishful eye
To Canaan's fair and happy land,
Where my possessions lie.
No chilling winds, nor pois'nous breath
Can reach that healthful shore;
Sickness and sorrow, pain and death,
Are felt and feared no more.

But the last seven chapters of Deuteronomy should forever disabuse that notion. Life with God is never so easy, so settled for any of us. Not for the Hebrews then and not for us living today. The pilgrim must ever progress, uphill, meeting new enemies around every bend.

The Prince of Egypt captures well Moses' humanity: his reluctance, his anguish, his developing sense of human justice and compassion that will serve him well in fulfilling God's task. What we learn of him in Deuteronomy is human as well: his unstinting realism in the face of a generation who failed to remember their parents' oppression and pain and the power of their God.

Moses was the single greatest realist about life with God. A proto-prophet, he gave God's message to the people and never diluted or belied it. A proto-priest, he represented the people to God with passion, conviction, and love. He made no promises of easy, happy endings—his own life had none—yet never did he look back with regret. The luxuries of Egypt and the solitary comfort of a nomad's life had both lost their appeal. He belonged with his people and with his God, the One he had come to know as a friend, face-to-face.

"The LORD is compassionate and gracious, slow to anger, abounding in love" (Ps. 103:8 NIV), wrote a psalmist years later, quoting the sacred *Shema* that Moses had first given to his people. It became a prayer that is still prayed every morning and every evening by Jews around the world. God has bound His love in a covenant, so that even though emotions will rise and fall, in the end the love will always prevail.

He will not always accuse,
nor will he harbor his anger forever . . .

For as high as the heavens are above the earth,
so great is his love for those who fear him;
as far as the east is from the west,
so far has he removed our transgressions from us.

As a father has compassion on his children,
so the LORD has compassion on those who fear him;
for he knows how we are formed,
he remembers that we are dust. (Ps. 103: 9, 11–14 NIV)

207

Dust, *Hapiru,* "the dusty ones," the old Egyptian slang word for the Hebrews—God remembers that we are dust. As Moses so clearly taught, evil is unpreventable and punishment inevitable. But we have a God who consciously forgets our sins, and consciously remembers our frailty. We have a God of grace, who loves all of us, even the dusty ones—especially the dusty ones, the meekest and the greatest.